Latter Days

Latter Days

A NOVEL

BASED ON THE SCREENPLAY BY C. JAY COX,
ADAPTED BY T. FABRIS

alyson books
los angeles

MANUFACTURED IN THE UNITED STATES OF AMERICA.

THIS TRADE PAPERBACK ORIGINAL IS PUBLISHED BY ALYSON PUBLICATIONS,
P.O. BOX 4371, LOS ANGELES, CALIFORNIA 90078-4371.
DISTRIBUTION IN THE UNITED KINGDOM BY
TURNAROUND PUBLISHER SERVICES LTD.,
UNIT 3, OLYMPIA TRADING ESTATE, COBURG ROAD, WOOD GREEN,
LONDON N22 6TZ ENGLAND.

FIRST EDITION: FEBRUARY 2004

04 05 06 07 08 a 10 9 8 7 6 5 4 3 2 1

ISBN 1-55583-868-5

CREDITS
COVER PHOTOGRAPHY BY CARL BARTEL.
COVER DESIGN BY BILLY EZELL.

The surface of the indoor pool glitters with flecks of silvery light. "Line up!" barks Coach Collins, the balding P.E. teacher. He wipes his moisture-dotted forehead with a hanky from his pants pocket while the next group of knob-kneed ninth-grade boys marches to the edge and begins to shake out their kinks. Pale flesh and bright-colored swimsuits blur in front of his eyes like he's seeing it all through a kaleidoscopic lens. *This is the last morning,* he promises himself, as he has for the last seven years. *No, really. No more daiquiri in a can. Not for breakfast anyway.*

Farron Davis's son, Aaron, the blond, lanky boy in lane 3, shifts anxiously in his yellow- and blue-striped Speedo. He shakes out his hairless thighs. He cranks his supple neck back and forth like a prizefighter. His face is taut, his clear blue eyes unwavering. So intense is his focus that he doesn't hear the shouts of spectators from the wobbly foldout aluminum bleachers—not even his older sister's "Come on, Aaron! You can do it!"

At 5 foot 10, Aaron is the tallest freshman swimmer for the Pocatello Indians. He is also the slowest.

Coach Collins raises his whistle. His hand trembles, poised in front of his lips. The swimmers crouch in unison. Aaron, who has until this point kept his vision trained on the concrete rim at the other end of the pool, finds himself glancing to his right to catch the eye of a broad-chested boy from Boise in lane 5.

The boy smiles.

The whistle shrieks. Aaron is the last one off the edge—another botched start—but as he penetrates the water it's as if his every sense is heightened. He feels the water envelop him, furl coolly up his fingers and over his wrists, wash across his head, over his shoulders, and down his back. For a split millisecond, he feels the last inch of air at his toes before they—along with the rest of him—submerge. And then, with a deafening roar in his ears, he swims. He swims like he never has before. It's like he's discovered something buried within himself—not strength, not technique, but a sense of pure freedom and oneness with the water that propels him right up with that Boise boy, the one whose brown eyes had stared at him with the same terror and the same dizzy thrill of recognition.

He swims with that boy like they're the only two in the pool.

When Coach Collins's vision clears, he can scarcely believe what he's seeing. *How can this slow kid from Pocatello be matching last year's Junior Olympic champion?*

Departure

A flashbulb went off in the Pocatello airport, illuminating the faces of a proud Idaho family. Blond sister, balding father, sweet mother in her Sunday best—and in the center of their huddled pose, standing tall in his fresh navy suit, was a filled-out and handsome Aaron Davis. At 19, he had matured into a stunning young man with broad shoulders, exquisite white skin, and blue eyes pale as an afternoon winter sky. His face reflected a sweet, trancelike joy—the glow of the Mormon missionary.

Aaron liked having his people crowded in around him. It was reassuring in the way that feeling a part of something always is. Airport photos: Families cozy up for the group hug, then separate as soon as the flash goes off. *Why not separate for the photo,* he wondered, *then stay together?* As they drifted away from him, blinking away their blind spots, he felt cut loose, deserted in a way that caught him by surprise.

His mother, Gladys, a small woman with orange hair and thick ankles, shuffled over to their volunteer photographer, a goateed college student who held out her camera like he couldn't wait to get rid of it. "Oh, thank you so much. You're just a sweetheart for doin' that." As she took it from him, she saw something that disturbed her and—

with a quick, deft motion—pinched the offending lint-ball from her rose-patterned skirt.

Aaron felt his sister, Susan, nudge him, and they shared a moment of bemused horror as they watched their mother fish high up under her skirt to hoist her sagging stockings.

"Oh, jeez, Mom," said Aaron. "You're flashing the whole terminal here."

"Well, I'm sorry, but if I don't hike 'em up, these things are gonna end up around my knees. I swear they aren't the same size anymore."

"Maybe *you're* not the same size..." suggested Susan, who was known for stating the obvious.

"Don't be ridiculous—I've been this size since I was a little girl!"

Susan and Aaron exchanged a look. As the only ones in the family who seemed to find anything funny, they were used to this method of communication and had it honed to a precision. A fluttered eyelash: *I'm bored.* A pursed pair of lips: *Try not to laugh.* A puff of air through flared nostrils: *Shock! But whatever you do, don't laugh.*

A woman's sterile voice reverberated off the beige walls of the terminal: "Your attention, please, final boarding for shuttle flight 57 to Salt Lake is now beginning. Ladies and gentlemen this is your final boarding call."

Aaron would have to take a bus from Salt Lake City down to Provo for his stay at the Mormon Training Center, a large network of buildings situated at the base of the steep-faced Wasatch mountain range. With its youthful inhabitants and its six-foot spear-tipped wrought-iron

gates, the center was sort of a cross between a college campus and a military training barracks. Aaron would spend
three weeks there, bunking in a small room with four
other would-be missionaries, readying himself for his two
years in Hollywood.

He still remembered that day in June when he was
called to serve. It was just two months ago that his mother had tearfully handed him the letter. He'd torn it open in
the living room—a form letter, but one whose words
seemed to shine off the page. "You are hereby called to
serve…" He often replayed it in his mind for inspiration:

*You are called to serve…as a missionary of The Church
of Jesus Christ of Latter-day Saints. You are…to labor in the
Hollywood California Mission…for a period of 24
months…report to the MTC in Provo on Wednesday, August
20, 2003. You will learn your discussions in English…*

The letter went on to say that he had been upheld as
one who was worthy to represent the Lord in delivering
the restored gospel, that he would be expected to maintain
the essential standards of conduct and appearance, that he
would be expected to keep the commandments, follow the
advice of his mission president, and live by mission rules.

Aaron knew living by mission rules would be no cake-
walk. Missionaries are expected to devote the entirety of
their time and attention to serving the Lord. They are not
allowed the distractions of computers, music, or movies.
The part about the movies had Aaron worried. He was a
real film freak, the kind who memorized entire scenes of

dialogue and who made it a point to know all sorts of trivia. Aaron was a big fan of the old black-and-white classics—Hitchcock films were his favorite. He'd probably seen *Psycho* 50 times.

Susan pulled Aaron into a tight hug, her shoulder-length hair soft against his cheek. He pressed his lips to her shoulder, burying his nose in the fibers of her fuzzy sweater and remembering how when they were kids she had mixed orange with yellow food coloring to dye the dog pumpkin for Halloween. Now she was starting as a chem major at BYU. "I'm losing the only other sane one around here," she whispered. "I'll miss you, bub."

As Susan backed up, Aaron's father stepped forward. He was a stern, wiry man with a military air about him. As Aaron tentatively opened his arms for a hug, the old man thrust out his hand instead. Aaron quickly pulled back and stretched out his own hand just as the father opened his arms. It was a comedy of errors—yet the two navigated the situation with grave seriousness. Finally, as their hands locked together, they settled on a stiff one-armed hug—far from optimal, but it would have to do. Farron Davis slapped his son's shoulder twice and averted his eyes. Then, grabbing him by the hand, he pressed a cool, round object into his palm.

"I believe this is yours now, son. Do us proud."

Aaron stared down at the antique silver pocket watch that had been carried by his father on his first mission—and by his grandfather, and by his grandfather's father before that. It felt heavy in his hand, like lead. Aaron met his father's eyes.

"Yes, sir. I will."

He stepped away. Where was his mother? He spotted her, hanging back, unable to look at him as she busied herself with her camera and pictures. "Mom," he said, and he opened his arms. She ran to him, and they embraced. "Well, now, honey, you just have yourself a real safe trip there and…and…oh, for cryin' out loud, I promised myself I wasn't gonna do this!" She pulled back, holding him at arm's length as her moist eyes lingered on his missionary-cropped hair, his rosebud mouth, his blond lashes…

"Mom, you promised. 'Cause if you start, then I will…"

She let go, fumbled with a handful of Polaroids, found one that satisfied her, and then tucked it into the front left pocket of his shirt. She pressed the photo against his chest. "You keep us right here, close to your heart, now, son." She tenderly straightened his collar. Aaron hugged her again as tears ran down his cheeks. So many feelings were coming up: fear mixed with exuberance, abandonment crossed with joy—and always a lingering measure of self-doubt. Was he really a worthy Mormon? Or was he somehow secretly deficient? And in keeping these doubts to himself, was he lying to his bishop? But whatever doubts Aaron may have had, he felt certain that there were truths ahead of him, truths that would make him a better man.

"I can't help it," sobbed Gladys. "It's just that you're my…you're my baby. You always will be."

That same Wednesday evening, in the lower hills of Hollywood, in a Spanish bungalow courtyard surrounded by moonlit palms and white eucalyptus trees, a sharply dressed Quinn hesitated at the door of apartment 3B. This was the first date he'd had in a long time and, despite his preppy good looks and hefty trust fund, he found himself mired in a mini confidence crisis. *Do I look like a dork? Are my shoes too casual?* Quinn smoothed his sandy-brown hair, checked his gray corduroy blazer for smudges, and was resisting the urge to adjust his "joint"—as he always crudely put it—when he noticed the lewd shadow of a small potted cactus plant jutting large across the stucco. It must be an omen, he decided, a reminder of his unflagging virility and an excuse to toss aside his fear. Quinn knocked. The door swung inward.

Oh, shit, thought Quinn. This was not what he had expected.

He squinted at the tall figure standing—no, *posing*—in the shadows: shirtless, tanned, hips cocked seductively in threadbare jeans, and with one long, muscular arm braced casually against the doorjamb. Christian William Markelli was clearly one of the beautiful. In a city full of 10s, an 11. Slicked-back, wavy dark hair. Mysterious brown eyes…

"Hey," said Christian.

"Hey," said Quinn.

The spring-green walls were dimly lit by a handful of white votive candles. A slow funky groove wafted from the stereo. Clearly the stage had been set. Skechers squeaking on the hardwood floor, Quinn entered in four short strides. "Nice apartment," he commented. "Where's…?" But he was unable to complete his sentence, because Christian closed the door, turned, lunged, and kissed him.

Quinn swooned under the pressure of Christian's lips, but then, recovering, he put his hands against that enormous shaved and sculpted chest and, with all his strength, he shoved.

Christian looked at him, perplexed and, yes, intrigued.

"Whoa, dude! What the fuck are you doing?" Quinn snapped. "I'm straight."

But Christian only laughed flirtatiously. His naked torso rippled under a shower of moonlight from the front window. His full lips beckoned like a force of nature. "That is so hot," he breathed, grabbing the lapels of Quinn's cord blazer, "when guys say that."

Quinn wormed free. "No," he said. "I'm serious, dude."

Christian edged forward, sliding his hands into his pockets, and voluptuously shimmying his unfastened jeans another few inches below the waistband of his yellow Calvin Kleins. The man was like a walking, breathing billboard ad. "Really?" he asked, tracing his fingers up the deep groove of his abs. "Never done it with a guy?"

"No!"

"Never got really drunk with the frat brothers in college and sort of…uh…let yourself go?"

"No!"

"No circle jerk at summer camp?"

"No…n-not really."

Christian hovered near Quinn. "Well, that's too bad." He fingered the antique brass key at his throat. "'Cause I'm amazing."

"Oh, really?"

"Yeah. Unlike most women, gay men don't do it to be

polite. I mean, I don't like to brag, but I could suck the engine block through the tailpipe of a '58 Chevy."

"Really?" said Quinn.

"Yeah. One of the big ones. I'm talkin' a 380."

"Oh. So, y-you know cars?"

"Yeah." Christian cocked his finger at him. "And beer. Unlike being with a woman, you and I can just crack a couple open right after. Hell, you can even have one during."

"Really?"

"Yeah, man, and you won't have to cuddle or talk about your feelings. This can be just a little fun between buddies."

"A little fun b-between buddies?" Quinn's tongue felt parched. He swallowed hard.

Christian moved his face up close, his dark hair falling into puppy-brown eyes, his pink tongue showing its skill and pliability as he pronounced each word: "And you'll never have to…call…me."

The sound of Quinn's yanked-down zipper roared through the quiet, moonlit apartment.

"Till you're up for another round, that is."

A row of buttons leapt in all directions, skittering across the floor as Christian ripped off Quinn's shirt and slowly tongued his way down the trembling straight boy's abs. *Wow*, he thought. *This Str8curious guy is something else. He has the drill down pat. And this preppy costume is hilarious.* His eyes darted to the clock and he noted the time—8:11—which was more or less five minutes after he had opened the door and two minutes shy of his record. But despite coming up shy, Christian would never disappoint a date—especially not one who was such a great actor. He intended to give Str8curious his "special"—the blow job to end all blow jobs.

Naked, they tumbled to the red Ikea sofa. Quinn's legs flung apart as he fell back, one of them bumping a polyurethane vase of yellow tulips off the heart-shaped coffee table. The vase clattered against the floor, spewing day-old tulip water across the pink throw rug.

Christian performed like an Olympic swimmer in the 200-meter butterfly, rising and falling, surfacing and submerging. And as the moon trained its spotlight on one side of his body, the candles made love to the other, casting their flames higher and brighter to accent the muscles of his back and ass. Beads of sweat sparkled like diamonds as they flew from the ends of his hair.

Quinn didn't even know which way his joint was pointing anymore, because it was going in a million directions at once. He no longer knew how big his joint was, or where it ended and the stranger's mouth began. Sure, he felt good. But he knew he'd feel even better—if he could just let go. His joint had become a whole new universe, and Quinn stood shaking at the door of that universe, feeling the throb of the music beyond. Ecstasy was waiting, if he could only forget…if he could only just step in…

Quinn stepped in.

"Oh!" he barked. "Oh, God! Oh, God! Oh, God!"

The exhausted candles suddenly grew dim. Christian stood, turned, and dabbed a finger at the corner of his mouth before flopping down next to Quinn on the sofa.

Quinn gasped and looked randomly about the room.

His eyes flitted from—but did not fully register—the framed, tie-dyed rainbow flag on the wall behind him, to the sky-blue furry cushion under his arm, to the nouveau-deco Miró-print chair. He started to speak, but he had no ability. So instead, he just let his head loll back against the sofa.

Where am I?

There. At least thoughts were coming now.

He groaned, pushing air from his lungs. His furry chest was drenched in sweat.

Yowza.

The lobotomy was a complete success.

Christian lumbered up and clomped barefoot to the fridge. He returned with a few cans of icy-cold Miller, flipped one open, licked a nice frosty splash of foam from his wrist, then handed the beer to Quinn.

Wow. Quinn took it with a no-questions-asked look of wonder and appreciation. Christian opened the other can and sat next to him. They each took a manly swig.

"Wow," said Quinn. "That was…wow."

"I know," said Christian. "Told you we'd have a beer."

Quinn laughed. "Aren't you even worried about Elizabeth walking in?"

"Elizabeth?"

"Yeah, man. I'm here for my date with Elizabeth."

Christian sat up. "Oh, no," he said. "Dude, you washed up on the wrong shore. My roommate is Julie—and she's in Malibu for the weekend. Elizabeth is at 3D—as in 'down the walk.' This is bungalow 3B, as in"—he stifled a smirk—"'blow job.' You're not Str8Curious from AOL?"

The two men shared an awkward moment.

Quinn dressed quickly. He grabbed his beer and headed for the door. As he hurried down the walkway, he allowed himself a quick glance back at bungalow 3B.

B, as in "blew his mind."

The moon had climbed higher in the navy-colored sky, and the cactus shadow had shrunk to the size of a truffle. A woman cleared her throat. Quinn turned. His date, Elizabeth, stood with her arms crossed on the porch of 3D.

When the door closed and Christian was alone, he experienced the familiar pain of something he could never quite bring himself to acknowledge—before he buried his head in his hands and groaned, "Not again."

Lila's

Dressed in standard-issue work uniforms—black trousers, white shirts, black aprons, and black ties—Christian and Julie were a vision of service professionalism as they took their habitual gossip break at the polished-maple order counter that divided Lila's kitchen. On one side, amid clanking pots and the explosive spray of the dishwashers, Carlos, the square-headed chef, ruled his prep cooks with an iron fist. On the other side, the waiters and waitresses slacked off shamelessly, gossiping and clowning around while they poured ice water, sliced lemons, and assembled salads at the stainless steel–legged chopping block. They were all still waiting for that one big break and intended to have fun while they were doing it.

Julie was not just Christian's roommate and coworker—she was his best friend and basketball buddy. A cute but tenacious young singer, she wore very little makeup and silver hoop earrings, and had pulled-back licorice braids. Her understated style may have had something to with her overstated mother, Marla, a meticulously put-together Malibu divorcée who was also the first black actress to win the People's Favorite Award for a role on a television soap opera. From the time Julie was a little girl, her mother had told her that success was only 10% talent,

30% hard work, and the rest was "who you know and what you look like."

Julie had decided to prove her mother wrong.

Unfortunately, so far she hadn't done that yet.

"Shut up!" she told Christian. "You are so lying to me."

"Nuh-uh. Check my journal." Christian pulled a Palm PDA from his pocket. He'd kept what he referred to as a "journal of conquests" since the winter before when a love-struck bank executive had bought him the handheld as a Christmas gift. "Go ahead. Check the entry for August 20."

"How do you work this crazy thing?" She fumbled with the buttons.

"No, no...like this." He removed the stylus and poked it at her. "See, maybe that's why you never got a second date with Brian. You're not even interested in long pointy things." He tapped an entry, then handed it back to her.

"Look, you ass, it was Brian who never got a second date with me." Julie's features lit up blue as she held her petite nose to the screen. "OK, here it is: August 20. Uh-huh. Oh, my God. That is so funny. 'This is bungalow 3B—as in blow job.'" She smacked the unit back into his hand. "And you say this was the second time it happened with one of Elizabeth's Internet hookups?"

"Yup—still think it's a coincidence she gave notice on the 21st? Honey, what more do you want?"

Julie tossed her thick ponytail as she walked over to a giant bowl of mixed greens. "Damn," she said grinning. "Those Midwest girls are so territorial."

Carlos put up half of Christian's order, and Christian snatched a handful of fries from the plate.

"You're bad, man," said the chef. He clomped off shaking his bulky head.

"Hey, Julie"—Christian stopped chewing for a second—"you should write a song about me and that guy."

She frowned. "Let's see, something like…'Was That You I Blew by Accident?' That'll be a big hit!"

"Trust me, girl—that shit would fly on the Palm Springs party circuit. Anyway, I can't believe you're almost done with the demo and you haven't written anything about your best friend."

Julie set down a few chilled plates and picked up a pair of salad tongs. "And I can't believe that if a tree fell in the forest, it wouldn't have something to do with you."

The bartender, a thin, fastidiously groomed black man in his late 20s, whisked into the kitchen. Andrew had recently been touted by *L.A. Weekly* as one of the best bartenders in L.A., and he was fond of quizzing others on drink recipes. "Hey, Julie," he said, pointing at her on his way to the freezer. "Martinis—vodka or gin?"

"Gin. And you!" She aimed her salad tongs at him. "You can tell that friend of yours to go fuck himself!"

Andrew arched an eyebrow and tightened the knot of his tie. "I only have one friend who can actually do that, and I doubt you've met."

"You know exactly who I'm talking about—that bass player you set my band up with. We were just looking for someone to lay down some tracks. By the second song it was like my bra had grown hands."

Andrew drew himself up. "The bar staff bears no responsibility for heterosexual acquaintances."

"Hey!" Christian shouted to Carlos. "They wanted no mushroom on the filet. No, wait, just give it to me." He picked up the mignon and—something he would never have bothered to do without an audience—scraped the mushroom-heavy sauce onto the counter. His final flourish was to lick his finger clean.

"Ugh," groaned Andrew. He sliced into a lemon at the chopping block.

Carlos scowled, but he was smiling underneath. "You can wipe up that mushroom sauce too, Christian."

Suddenly a tall blur of auburn hair and hard-core New York attitude breezed up to the counter. " 'Scuse me, wanna-bes." She dinged the bell and turned away. "Order up!"

"Oh, ho, ho!" Christian laughed. "Look out, people. One callback, and she's Margo Channing."

"*Second* callback, thank you. Second lead in a *feature*." Traci shook her fist jubilantly. "I am so-o-o getting this part. Soon I can kiss all you losers goodbye and finally justify moving to this miserable fucking town." She squatted down to grab some water glasses and popped up in front of Andrew. She cocked her head at him. "Ever read for Barry Wolfe?"

Andrew smiled as a collective groan rolled through the kitchen.

Julie scrunched up her face. "Ew."

Christian shoved another handful of fries into his mouth. "Hey," he joked. "What's with skimping on the fries here? Come on, Carlos, load me up, man."

"Eh, go fuck yourself," Carlos laughed.

Traci glared at Christian through L'Oréal-thickened

eyelashes. She loved him, but his frivolity often wore on her. She moved toward the door but did a complete about-face when he added, "Barry Wolfe read me once for this commercial. He was licking me with his eyes the whole time."

Andrew snorted. "They don't call him the 'Wolfe Who Cried Boy' for nothing. You know, he wouldn't even see me for that crappy TV wacky gay neighbor thing."

Julie picked up her salads. "What's that about?"

"Hell, yeah, I'm gay...I'm wacky."

"Maybe you're not neighborly," Traci suggested.

Andrew pointed his knife at her, an impaled lemon wedge leaking juice at its tip. "Fuck you," he said, laughing. "I'm Donna Reed on a stick."

"Excuse me, darlings," came a pleasant, polished voice. Christian hopped away from the counter to stand at attention. The proprietress had entered quietly from the depths of the kitchen, appearing—in her rich tailored suit and seductively unbuttoned white blouse—much younger than she really was. Her long brown hair still shone like a pampered starlet's, and her green eyes still flashed with mystery and appeal. Despite her years out of the business, Lila Montagne—yes, *that* Lila Montagne—still carried herself like a pro. Lila crossed her arms and enunciated tersely: "I hate to interrupt this important discussion among all you big sta-a-ars."

"I'll settle for medium star," joked Christian.

"Point well taken—but in the meantime, I hear Disney is opening a Fantasia restaurant, in which the plates fly themselves to the table. Until then, what to do?"

The waiters accepted the gentle reprimand, grabbed up their orders, and scurried off to deliver them.

Christian lowered his head and turned a half-circle before plunging assward through the double doors. "Hot stuff," he shouted. "Comin' through!"

"That's the spirit," said Lila.

Arrival

A brown blanket of smog.

A vast, glowing mass of dots—all jumbled and disconnected.

This is what Aaron Davis saw from his window as his plane circled in a holding pattern over Los Angeles. He brushed the crumbs of peanuts from the lap of his navy slacks.

It had been a long three weeks in Provo.

Thirty minutes later, Aaron stepped out into "the white zone," for passenger loading and unloading only. If some men's faces were carved from granite, Aaron's was carved from soap—Ivory soap, 99.9% pure. He stood on the platform, disoriented, but with brave posture, like a plastic groom on top of a cake, his two small suitcases on the concrete beside him, his navy blue tie tucked under the black strap of his church-sanctioned proselytizing shoulder bag—purchased at the Missionary Training Center for $30—which crossed his chest like a military sash.

The shoulder bag contained a copy of the Bible, *The Book of Mormon, The Missionary Handbook*—commonly known as "The White Bible" among missionaries—and the six discussions he had studied over the last three weeks at the Missionary Training Center. His name tag—a black rectangle of plastic issued on his first day at the training center—was affixed to the left side of his shirt. Its white lettering spelled out ELDER DAVIS, HOLLYWOOD MISSION, CHURCH OF THE LATTER-DAY SAINTS.

He would wear it everywhere.

A black Ford Saturn sedan pulled up. From the car two handsome and wholesome-looking youths in black suits—assistants to the Mission president—emerged with identically bland expressions.

The A.P.'s, Aaron thought. *They're here for me.*

"Elder Davis? Hi, I'm Elder Smith. This is Elder Burton."

"Hi there."

His hand was shaken firmly, his suitcases loaded into the trunk, and the rear passenger side door opened for him, then closed. Aaron inspected the car's interior. The gray upholstery was weathered and worn but smelled new—like some indefinable brand of soap-scented air freshener.

Aaron could not find his seat belt.

The driver, Smith, a tall, skinny youth with strawberry-blond hair and big ears, swung his head around. "Are you comfortable, Elder Davis?"

"Yes, thank you. I'm…fine."

"Good."

"But I can't find my seat belt."

"What?" said Burton from the front passenger seat.

"He says he can't find his seat belt," said Smith.

The front doors swung open on either side of the car as the A.P.'s climbed out and came around to help.

"Did you stick your hand in there?" asked Burton, a stocky youth with the whitest teeth Aaron had ever seen.

"Yeah," said Aaron.

"Really? Try again—it should be there," suggested Smith.

Aaron reached self-consciously through the opening between seat and backrest. A cold metal object brushed his fingertips with maddening proximity. "I can't get it."

Smith unbuttoned the cuff of his dress shirt. "OK, here," he said, then reached across Aaron's lap, plunging his hand into the dark crevice with a determined ferocity. Immediately the back of the car filled with the odor of cologne and suit sweat. As Smith fished around, the starched seam of his crotch pressed against Aaron's thigh.

Aaron sucked in his breath.

"Thanks, Davis—you're making it easy on me. Here ya go." Smith pulled out the seat belt, clicked the two parts together, and jerked it tight across Aaron's lap. It was a gesture that could have meant anything.

"Thanks," said Aaron.

Smith patted his knee—"Don't mention it, Greenie"—and closed the door.

"Greenie" was the affectionate nickname for all new missionaries.

Click-pa, click-pa—the big-eared Smith had flipped on his turn signal. Aaron put his forehead to the window and looked out in amazement. Everybody seemed late for something. A woman was shouting into her cell phone as she ran through the crosswalk tugging a huge stack of baggage on a flimsy aluminum cart. A man wearing a turban and blue rhinestone-studded cowboy boots was hurling suitcases into the back of his cab. A cluster of serious-looking Chinese businessmen wandered up to the missionaries' car, peered in at Aaron questioningly, and then moved on. Smith had barely begun to inch away from the curb when five roaring blue-and-yellow shuttle buses careened past. The car rocked back and forth on its tires, paralyzed and bewildered by the dark cloud of exhaust.

Aaron closed his eyes. *Lord, please help me—I've landed in the middle of chaos.*

Seconds later, an ebb in the flow of traffic supervened, and Elder Smith carefully pulled from the curb. Aaron was fascinated by the color-shifting columns of light on display. As they swung past, he turned to look out the back window just in time to see a tall, pale-blue cylinder turn foggy gray, then melt into vibrant red. Facing forward he watched the green road signs: CENTURY BLVD., SEPULVEDA NORTH. At the end of the ramp a homeless man—black with grime, in pants so long they covered his feet—stood roadside in a dark hooded sweatshirt. His swollen paws held a large, hand-printed sign that bobbed and bucked against the wind:

WELCOME

TO

HELL

In the glare of the sedan's headlights, the man's eyes glowed like fiery coals.

Smith guided the steering wheel hand over hand as the car veered onto the freeway.

"Hope you're ready for L.A., kid."

Mellow lighting.

White linen tablecloths.

Burnished wood.

Potted palms.

Oriental fans.

Dusty tapestries.

This is what Christian William Markelli saw five out of seven nights per week, on his shift at Lila's, where the martini was back and the ghosts of Hollywood had never left.

It was a fairly busy night for a Thursday. Christian hurried forward with an armful of plates loaded with classic Hollywood fare—one spaghetti and meatballs, a medium-rare filet, turkey cordon bleu, and a Cobb salad. On his way through the dining area, he passed Julie punching in some drink orders at the bar.

"Hey," said Julie. "What you doin' tonight?"

"Depends," answered Christian. "What *you* doin'?"

"I'm taking one of my tracks over to Funny Boy. It's diva karaoke night."

"Aw, Julie…" he whined. "Karaoke?"

"They've also got two-for-one margaritas."

"I'll be there."

Christian moved on past the curved mahogany bar through the outer door to serve one of the small cozy tables on the patio. It was a lovely night. The air was warm and crisp. He removed the last dish from his forearm, whipped out his pepper mill, and was twisting it briskly over a woman's Cobb salad when a black Ford Saturn pulled up to the stoplight. As if tapped on the shoulder, Christian turned from the table to meet the soulful blue eyes of a young man with cropped hair peeking out at him through the half-open backseat window.

Seconds passed. Neither man looked away. The light switched to green. The sedan moved off.

Christian—only slightly aware of the intensity of his feelings—shrugged.

"Can I get you anything else, sir? Would anyone like another drink?"

Julie sang like an angel that night, while Christian, Traci, and Andrew downed margarita after margarita. Unfortunately, they were the only people in the club.

Birds perched on power lines twittered and chirped through the early Friday traffic sounds as Aaron happily soaked up this hazy-cloudy morning. So this was where he'd be living? Sweet. Swinging his stack of boxes, he took the last two steps leading into the lush, cheerful courtyard and stopped.

"Green!" shouted Ryder. The slight senior missionary staggered up behind him with a load of boxes that went well over his head, though all of them were fairly light. "You mind if we keep it movin'?"

"Sorry," said Aaron. "No problem."

"That's good," said Ryder. "'Cause those mattresses still need unloading, and we don't have all day."

Every new missionary—the "greenie," or just plain "green"—is paired with a senior missionary, someone who knows the routine and can show him the ropes. A skinny but scrappy little guy from American Fork, the 19-year-old Elder Ryder had been out in the field for six months. To Aaron, he seemed kind of bitter for someone who was supposed to be serving the Lord—but it was only his first day in the field, so what did he know? Missionary companions were never to be out of each other's sight. Aaron and Ryder would proselytize together, pray together, eat together, bunk together, exercise together—basically do everything but use the bathroom together.

Right then, though, the two were moving boxes together. And when they finished with these, they would start grabbing furniture.

Aaron staggered off along the walkway. He looked up to see a fat dove staring at him from a power line. A telephone trilled from someone's window.

In the middle of a room with red-painted walls, a massive, immobile lump snored loudly into his pillow, the faint call of a phone barely audible through his dream. But on the third ring, the lump stirred, extending from under its cream-colored sheets what appeared to be a long muscular arm. And on the fourth ring, the lump turned over and lifted his head. Christian's partied-out eyes were swollen into slits. His hair was a dark, matted mass. He dropped his hand repeatedly in the direction of the phone, and when his hand finally landed on it, threw the phone to his ear, where it clonked against his skull.

"Ow! Fuck!"

"Yeah?" came a laughing woman's voice. "Fuck you too."

"Is that you, Mom?"

"No, it's Julie. Where the hell are you?"

"I'm here. Isn't this where you called me?" Christian sat up gingerly, holding his head. "Where the hell did we end up last night?"

"I don't know, but I woke up without my bra. That's never a good sign."

"Woke up without your..." Christian glanced down to discover a strip of stretched black lace bound tightly across his pecs. "I wouldn't worry about it. Hey, why are you calling me anyway—and not just tiptoeing across the hall with sympathy and Excedrin?"

"I tried that, but when I knocked on the door there was no answer. You must've been out cold. I thought you'd already gone. Hey, spin class is starting. I'm calling on my cell."

Christian suddenly remembered his commitment. "Oh, fuck." He rolled out of bed and staggered to the bathroom. When he unhooked Julie's bra it shot off him like a rubber band, lost its aerial momentum after a few feet, and then dropped with a splash into the toilet. "Ugh," he groaned, reaching down into the bowl. The dripping black lingerie reminded him of when he was 7 and his dad sent him trout fishing with Uncle Bob. The pit of his stomach roiled with an identical disgust.

Ten minutes later, in running shoes, his favorite tight blue shorts, and a white muscle shirt, his black hair slicked with finishing gloss, his eyes shaded by Fendi, and his bra trauma forever suppressed from his memory, our hung-over hunk hero stumbled out the door and broke into a light jog. Three strides forward and—*bonk*—he ran right into an extra-firm twin-size mattress. Catching his balance, he came face-to-face with a sleepy-faced cutie in baggy jeans and a gray T-shirt, who recovered his end of the mattress with a squeeze that revealed his powerful shoulders. Christian was stunned. What was it that was so attractive about him? The way he blushed? The way his cropped blond hair looked like a sprouted plant on top?

"Sorry," Aaron said, and he said it like he meant it.

Christian was charmed yet—*Have I fucked this one?*—puzzled. He pulled off his sunglasses. "We've met!"

"What? No, I'm brand-new here."

"Hey, Greenie, let's get a move on, huh?" A cranky-looking youth craned his bird-like neck around the other end of the mattress.

"Sorry, I g-gotta go," said the cute blond reluctantly.

Christian glanced up ahead of them to see two massive football jocks lugging one of the butt-ugliest couches he'd ever seen across the threshold of Elizabeth's old apartment.

"What the…?"

Welcome to the Neighborhood

There were no "empties"—no beer cans used as makeshift ashtrays—cluttering up the coffee table. There were no porn mags—*Hustler, Playboy,* or *Maxim*—lying around in brazen piles or guiltily tucked under a mattress. Not a single bong, nor rolling papers, nor stinking Baggie of weed would ever cross the threshold. No Coke or Pepsi chilling in the fridge. No coffeemaker dripping out its wake-me-up aroma from the kitchen countertop. Still, with its hand-me-down mismatched furniture, its total lack of decor, and its definitively male odors—from aftershave to nylon sock fungus to that territorial cloud of urine musk near the bathroom—the inside of 3D (as in recently *D*-parted by Elizabeth) was already starting to feel like your typical frat house.

Straight away, the puce sofa in the center of the living room spoiled any hope of an attractive living environment. Aaron regarded its frayed upholstery, the puff of foam leaking out the inside seam of one arm. It was early afternoon, just after lunch, and a mild breeze wafted through the doorway. Elders of the newly formed missionary household—Davis, Ryder, Harmon, and Gilford—were busy arranging church-donated furniture and other odd supplies.

Aaron tried to suppress a sneeze as he emptied out a must-infused duffel bag. He pulled out a handful of books from one end and placed them eye-level on a shelf. The titles were so dusty they were barely legible. He swiped his wrist across the spines. But the topics—*Mormon Answer to Skepticism, The New Mormon History,* and *The Mormon Hierarchy*—failed to excite him. Delving back into the bag, he watched Ryder shoving a box across the floor with his foot.

"Hey, Elder Ryder, you're kicking that thing like you have something against it."

"So?" said Ryder, pushing the box under an old desk.

"So you're not going to unpack it?"

Ryder looked at Aaron. Without a word, he reached under the desk, slid the box back out, and dropped to one knee beside it. Maintaining eye contact as he pulled open the bottom drawer of a four-tiered metal filing cabinet, he then picked up the box with his skinny, straining arms and dumped in an avalanche of dilapidated old maps, dried-up fountain pens, file folders, and recycled notebooks.

"Nice," said Aaron.

"All unpacked...Mrs. Kravitz."

Ryder tossed the box aside, fell back into an ugly forest-green beanbag chair, and went into a surly trance, chewing his thin lips vigorously as his thumb worked a stress ball that was apparently supposed to look like Bill Clinton's head.

Aaron didn't get it. Ryder's personality fit the Mormon Church's teachings like a square peg in a round hole. The guy was a constant grouch.

Moments later, Harmon—a well-built 21-year-old with alert brown eyes and a cauliflower ear—swaggered in from the bedroom wearing loose-fitting jeans and a threadbare chocolate-colored T-shirt. Having toed the line for months, the former state-champion wrestler was just 60 days from going home and had a bad case of the stir-crazies. "Final bell," he groaned, "Harmon goes down." Eyes shut, tongue stuck out sideways, he flung his huge body facedown onto the sofa, raising a small cloud of dust and microfilaments. "Hey, Gilford!" he called out, squirming sensuously into a position of complete comfort. "Why don't you come on over here and give me a back rub?"

Gilford strode in behind him. Even bigger than Harmon and a backup linebacker during his first year at BYU, he crackled with the same testosterone-amped energy. Gilford had Son of Zion Machismo Syndrome. He was very serious about his masculinity. "Wrong tree," he said. "Barkin'—if you think I'm rubbin' your pimply back, ya homo." He reached into an open box for some wads of newspaper, which he shot one by one with exaggerated form into a small wicker wastepaper basket.

Harmon lifted his head. "What about you, Davis? C'mon, Greenie, help a guy out, huh?"

Aaron made himself look busy. "I think I have stuff to put away."

"OK, OK…fine. Be that way." Harmon rolled off the sofa. "Gilf! Buddy!"

Gilford shook his bristly blond head disgustedly. "No way, man."

"Ten minutes. You know I'd give *you* a backrub." Suddenly, he jumped up to block one of Gilford's newspaper wads.

"Bro," said Gilford, nose-diving onto the sofa. "You're on!"

"No way, I asked you first."

"Nope," said Gilford.

Harmon took a running start, pounced like a tiger, and landed with the full weight of his elbow buried between his missionary companion's shoulder blades. "How 'bout some deep tissue work?"

"Aargh! That hurts!" Gilford kicked Harmon off. "You jerk!"

Harmon roared with laughter, leap-frogged wildly over Ryder's head, and dove into the bedroom. The sound of his large feet hammering the floor was like something you'd hear at a construction site.

Gilford was a graceful blur as he ran after him. "Prepare to die, dude."

"Hey," said Ryder, hunkering down into his beanbag. "Sheesh. What a coupla fags."

Just then, there was a knock at the front door. Aaron trotted over and opened it to find the guy who'd bumped into his mattress that morning. Wavy black hair, brown eyes, dazzling smile…

Aaron crammed his hands into his pockets. "Hi."

"Hi," said Christian. He was hiding something behind his back. "Remember me from across the way?"

"Oh, yeah. Hi." Aaron's attraction became shame before he even had a chance to recognize it—so he panicked. "Harmon!"

Harmon and Gilford—their T-shirts damp from roughhousing—bounded into the room. They froze five feet from the doorway like a pair of alerted watchdogs. Whoever this flauntingly sexual being standing in the doorway was, he may as well have been the devil.

Tall, buff, and as uniformly tan as a Chippendale stripper, Christian had draped his ripped torso in a cream-colored sweater vest with chocolate-brown piping. His powder-blue mini shorts accentuated his well-developed thighs, but the bright white laces that crisscrossed football-style up the front of his fly drew four sets of sex-starved male eyes to his bulge. As if his clothing weren't foreign enough, Christian's body language communicated something even more unnerving—an obvious willingness to have sex with men.

Smiling like he expected love and gratitude to come showering down on him at any moment, Christian swung forth his gift. "I brought you guys a little welcome-to-the-complex sixer."

The missionaries stared dully at the six-pack.

Christian wiggled it in front of them at arm's length, not getting it. *Who are these yo-yos? Why doesn't somebody take it?* "There's a lime tree across the street," he added, gesturing with his thumb.

"Uh, thanks, but we don't drink," said Aaron.

"Huh? What kind of frat boys are you?"

"We're not frat boys," said Ryder. "You got the wrong apartment, buddy."

"We're Mormons," Aaron explained. "We're doing a mission here."

"Really?" Suddenly Christian looked like he was deciding whether to spit or swallow. "Hey, you almost had me going…there…" His voice trailed off as the truth sunk in. "Well, OK. Guess I'll see you guys around." He shut the door.

Left alone, the missionaries performed various pack-like gestures of territory. Ryder shrugged his bony shoulders and scowled from his beanbag. Harmon scratched his groin, then snorted in disgust. "Whoa," said Gilford, smelling his own armpit.

But Aaron found himself blushing, and to hide it he bent over a box.

Christian meandered across the courtyard. *Mormon missionaries,* he thought, *how totally bizarre.* He pictured the cute one, his cropped blond hair and snub nose. *We're Mormons. We're doing a mission here.* What a refreshingly simple message. Christian laughed. It was a light laugh, a little crush-laugh—but then, as he moved across the courtyard, a voice stabbed out at him through the window.

"Wow. Who called up Deliver-a-Fag?"

"Jeez, Ryder, can you be a little louder? He can probably hear you."

"I don't care. Did you see those flippin' shorts he was wearing?"

Christian looked down at the shorts he'd purchased at the Gaymart on Santa Monica Boulevard the week before. OK, maybe they *were* a bit brief. But they had their butch elements—what about those wide navy stripes down the sides? And wasn't the crotch laced up like those pants they wear in the NFL? A sense of outrage settled in his throat.

His pace quickened, and he did a slow burn as he entered his apartment. *Flippin'? What kind of word is flippin'? And what the fuck is wrong with my flippin' shorts?*

Thin tips of shoulder blades visible through his slightly sweaty white shirt, Andrew, the bartender, restocked after closing. Julie, Traci, and Christian, their ties loosened, sat slouched at the bar, folding piles of freshly laundered crimson cloth napkins into decorative fans. Christian threw a couple of unorthodox "origami" swans and a frog into the mix and, bored, picked up his frog and a swan to act out a little dialogue. The other waiters ignored him. They were used to his distractions.

"Psst. Hey, froggie. Want some beer?" said the swan-napkin.

"We don't flippin' drink beer," said the frog-napkin.

"Why not?" asked the swan.

"We're too uptight."

Wrapped in an elegant Japanese print–pattern silk jacket, Lila approached the bar with her usual silent stealth. She pulled up behind Christian and sidled up next to him.

Suddenly sensing his boss's presence, Christian jumped and tried to hide his puppets. But Lila was oblivious.

"So, Christian…"

"Yes?"

"There is the most adorable man, Daniel, here this evening." She snuggled her arm around him and placed her lips close to his ear. "I thought I might introduce the two of you."

"Really?" said Christian, turning devilishly to touch foreheads with her. "Blue shirt? End of the bar?"

"Actually, yes."

Christian brought out his PDA, then punched a few buttons. "Ssss. Daniel...I think we've met. August 3, I believe...uh, yep. Here it is. Not so good. Nope." He frowned, looking regretfully at her. "Not so good."

Lila sighed, shrugged, and with an upraised finger leaned across the bar. "Andrew, would you be a love and pour me a glass of that merlot there?"

"Sure thing." Andrew approached with the bottle, and slipped a folded Post-it across the bar. "And you also got a call from Ben, Miss M."

"I see. Thank you." Lila seemed suddenly distraught. She took the Post-it, tucked it into her pocket, and—as Andrew poured the merlot—slipped down from her bar stool. "Well," she said with fragile bravado. "I suppose if he's going to call this late in the week, I'm justified in calling him this late in the evening, right?"

"Absolutely," said Andrew, extending her glass.

Lila accepted it by the stem, and then raised it, saying, "Cheers." Then she smoothly drifted off to make her call.

"Cheers," said Christian absently.

Her departure produced an exchange of raised eyebrows, but that's as far as it went. Gossiping about the boss was forbidden on the grounds of the establishment—not that this would stop any of them from doing so once they hit the sidewalk.

"Oh, oh, oh," said Christian. "Wanna hear something freaky?"

His three friends leaned in. Of course they did.

"You remember those four guys who moved into Elizabeth's old apartment? Guess what they do."

"Quadruplet porn stars," Andrew said dryly.

"In this town?" said Julie. "Hardly freaky."

Traci slapped the bar. "I know, they're rodeo clowns!"

"No," said Christian. "It's even weirder than that. They're Mormon missionaries. Swear to God."

Andrew made a face. "Ugh."

"Although ya gotta admit..." mused Traci, gazing down at her napkin fan, "rodeo clowns would be cool."

"Wow," said Andrew. "Mormon missionaries, huh? Well, they must love *your* aberrant lifestyle. I dated this Mormon guy once. His family put him through shock therapy."

"Shock therapy?" Christian bit his lip to keep from laughing.

"Yeah, and not just on your brain, man. I'm talking about on the private parts."

Christian released his lip. "You're shitting me."

"Strapped him down, showed him photos of naked men, then zapped the shit outta his wee-wee."

"And this made him straight?" Traci wrinkled up her nose.

"Oh, no," said Andrew. "He stayed gay, all right. Definitely fucked with his head though. We'd have sex, and the guy was a wild man. Then he'd try to throw himself out the window. One day he did."

"So what?" said Traci. "You live on the first floor."

"True, but it was still hell on my azaleas. Hey, Christian, wouldn't it be funny if you converted one of them instead of one of them converting you?"

Christian liked the idea. "Can you imagine?"

"Oh, no." Julie waved her hand. "I've seen these boys. They're wound way too tight for that."

"Yeah," said Traci. "No alcohol, no coffee, no cigarettes."

"No sex," added Andrew.

Julie scrunched up her face. "Now, that is harsh."

Traci shot Andrew a sly look. "Bet he can't do it."

"Wait, wait, wait!" Christian sat up straight. "Are we betting here?"

Julie jumped on it. "Same as always?" she proposed. "Five and a sixer?"

"Wait a sec," countered Andrew. "This is big. I got 20 bucks says he can."

"High stakes?" Traci smirked. "OK, 50 says he *can't*. I've seen those guys out pedaling their bikes—starchy long-sleeved shirts in 90-degree weather, their little satchels bobbing up and down... I'm thinking this time, baby, you have met your match."

"Bullshit!" Julie laughed. "Fifty says he *can,* and I bus tables for a week!"

Andrew jabbed his finger at her. "Fifty bucks and *two* weeks, *can't.*"

"OK," said Traci. "I'm in with Andrew. There's no way."

Julie put on her game face. "Cool. We on?"

Andrew lined up four shot glasses and pulled out a bottle of cinnamon schnapps. "OK, but there has to be a time line. I can't wait five years. He gets two months— after that, the deal's off."

"November 15? Sounds doable." Christian's face was

radiant at the prospect. "What are we saying here? I get one of them to do anything? Blow job, or…?"

"We need proof," said Traci.

"Of course," said Julie. "For our cynical New Yorker…"

"Not cynical," corrected Traci. "Practical."

Andrew finished pouring out the last shot of schnapps. "OK," he said. "Underwear. I knew this other Mormon guy in the army. They got these sacred boxers—they shimmer. Get me some of those."

Christian licked his lips. "Sacred undies? Get out. I gotta see this." He rubbed his hands together. "All right, I'm in. I can get one of those boys out of his underwear."

Traci raised her schnapps. "Seal the deal!"

"All right," said Christian, raising his glass along with the others. "So, are we going out tonight?"

"Oh, please," said Andrew. "Not another episode of 'Christian hooks up.'"

"Hey…" Christian suavely straightened his tie. "Gotta keep my skills honed."

"To skills," said Traci, extending her Schnapps.

"To sacred boxers," said Andrew.

A clink of glasses. They all drank.

Aaron wondered if he'd ever get any sleep on this mission. Ryder's snoring was like the sound of someone trying to start up a lawnmower. It didn't help that his bed was only two feet away. How did someone so puny make such a big sound? Aaron lay on top of his covers and tried not to imagine suffocating him with one of those lumpy church-donated pillows. That wouldn't be very Christlike.

He willed himself to imagine each roaring, sputtering snort as the dainty creak of tree branches in a gentle storm.

It didn't work. No storm, not even an ugly storm, sounded this terrible. If it was just the snoring, Aaron might have had a chance to pull it off. But no. Every three or four breaths, Ryder's lips made these tiny *plip* noises, like little kisses an old lady might give her cat. Aaron tried to turn them into rain sounds, drops falling into a small puddle near the window. But that didn't work either. He just kept imagining Ryder's thin, chewed-up lips and the viscous strands of saliva stretching between them as they formed that frightening sound. There was just no way around it.

Suddenly there was a noise outside. Voices. Footsteps. His teachers at the Missionary Training Center had advised him to be on guard for crime in Los Angeles. A noise outside ought to be investigated. If it wasn't his own bungalow being broken into, it could be someone else's. Still, he didn't want to feel like the town busybody, running to the living room window with a pair of binoculars in tow. Aaron decided to compromise. He went to the bedroom window, but he did not run. Instead, he used the silent gait he learned in Scouts—the hunter's stalk of the Pocatello Indians. Heel-toe, toe-heel, heel-toe, toe-heel…

The windowsill felt cool against his forearm. Aaron lowered his head and stuck his fingers between the shades, prying them open to peer into the dark courtyard.

Then he saw him—that gay guy who'd run into his mattress that morning.

The one who'd brought the beer.

His jeans and tight red T-shirt fit him more like a leotard than a set of clothes. Aaron gulped. It was almost
obscene.

He was juggling his keys on his front porch, and it was
taking him awhile. Was he drunk? There was a guy with
him, hovering near the door. A huge guy—massive chest,
thick arms—but with long, spindly legs. Aaron had seen a
lot of kids like that back at his high school gym in
Pocatello, and even some freshmen at BYU. They pumped
up their arms because it made them feel manly, but they
blew off the leg work. According to Harmon, wrestling a
buff guy on a pair of stilts was the easiest takedown of all.
They had no foundation.

Aaron looked harder. The guy's Levi's must've been a
size 20.

Finally his gay neighbor found the right key and got
the door open. He moved aside to let in the stilt man.

Promiscuous sex is rampant among homosexuals.

The words skirted through Aaron's mind, as if whispered by the ghost of Spencer W. Kimball. But Aaron was
more unnerved by what happened next. His neighbor
paused at the door, then turned his head and seemed to
look straight at him.

Aaron figured he probably couldn't be seen. All the
lamps were turned off in his room. And, thanks to the
moon and a few decorative fluorescents at the base of
some palm trees, it was pretty light outside. But he wasn't
certain. And when his neighbor cocked his handsome
head at him, eyes flashing as if to say "come on over and
join the party," Aaron literally felt the floor go out from

under him. When it came back, his neighbor was gone, bungalow 3B's door was shut, and Aaron turned away.

He had felt something terrible.

Probably he'd been dreaming. Yes, that must've been it. He had fallen asleep on his feet.

Aaron went back to bed, tried again to sleep through Ryder's snores, gave up, then stared at the ceiling until slowly the objects on his nightstand—his clock, *The Book of Mormon,* his mission journal, and a Polaroid photo propped against the lamp—were distinguishable in the soft light of dawn. Aaron rolled over, reached across to his nightstand, and picked up the dog-eared Polaroid his mother had tucked into his pocket at the airport. His hand tilted it to catch the light from the window.

They all looked happy.

Aaron stared at the photo. His nose sniffled, a small, sad sound.

Ryder tossed and raised his head. "Hey, for flip's sake, keep it down over there, will ya?"

Stormin' Mormon

Aaron had loved being at the Missionary Training Center in Provo. From the moment he stepped through its large glass entry doors, he'd felt a surge of excitement and a sense of purpose that were like nothing he'd ever experienced before. He loved the structure and routine of the place. From the time he woke up in the morning to the time he went to sleep, his every activity was scheduled: meals, prayers, individual and group study sessions, exercise, classes, even his daily shower. It allowed Aaron to focus on one thing: his relationship with God and his mission in serving him.

But Aaron had not had a typical experience. A disruptive incident occurred during his last week of training. Aaron and all the other missionary trainees were having supper in the main dining hall. Rows of cafeteria tables full of young men in white shirts with black name tags threw back glasses of milk and wolfed down Salisbury steak or turkey burgers. The walls echoed with the clack of trays, the jangle of silverware, and the rumble of low conversation broken up by flurries of laughter.

Aaron's companion Elder Cox held out a square yellow Post-it note to him. "Hey, Elder Davis. Look at this. Ever heard of the Stormin' Mormon?"

"Uh-uh," said Aaron. He took the Post-it and read, 'Elder Marx seems to have a little problem with skid marks. Someone should tell him—cleanliness is next to godliness. Signed, Stormin' Mormon the Post-it Prankster.' "

Aaron cracked up. "What is this?" Elder Marx was one of the sterner teachers at the training center.

"Let me see," said Elder Todd. "I saw one of those notes up in the bathroom." He took the Post-it from Aaron, read it, then spit a mouthful of milk across the table. Suddenly an eruption of laughter broke out. Someone tossed a piece of turkey burger bun.

"Who're you trying to kid, Elder Todd. We all know it's you!"

Elder Todd grinned ear to ear. "Maybe," he said. "Maybe not."

Elder Pead spoon-flipped a lima bean across the table at him. "You may be going to hell, Todd, but you sure are funny."

The next day more Post-its were left out in various places throughout the MTC: over the trash can in the bathroom, stuck to a desk in room 7, on the side of another elder's bunk. Each note alleged some silly quirk about another teacher. Some were cleverer than others, but none were very tasteful. By dinner time, once again the youthful sisters and elders were squirrelly with news of various Stormin' Mormon notes they'd found. Aaron was proud that it was one of his bunkmates who'd penned the day's entertainment.

But everything changed that night, when Elder Todd's

things were packed up for him and he was put on the next bus up to Salt Lake for a late-night flight back to Oregon. The next morning the MTC president addressed all the sisters and elders in the dining hall.

"What disturbs me most about this so-called prankster is that he seems to have gotten some kind of grassroots encouragement from the other missionaries in training here, and even his own bunkmates who should have been responsible for setting him straight. So, since this seems to have become a widespread insurrectionist mentality, let me just review a basic truth: Every priesthood leader, from the president of the church down to the president, zone leaders, and district leaders of the mission, are acting on behalf of God the Father and Jesus Christ." The president drew himself up and his watery eyes glared out across the dining hall. "The kingdom of God is not a democracy. It is a monarchy, with Jesus Christ as the king. Hence, disobedience—including disrespect—to your teacher, church leaders, and even to each other, is identical to disobedience to God and Jesus Christ. Is that understood?"

When the president had finished his speech, a shocked silence hung over the dining hall. No one felt as bad as Aaron and his two other bunkmates, Elders Clarkson and Pead.

That afternoon, classes were canceled so that all companion assignments throughout Todd's zone could be changed.

For the first two days after the incident, Aaron studied, prayed, and tried to make good. But as hard as he tried, he just didn't see what the big deal was with the whole Post-it Prankster scandal. Then, on the third day, one of the other elders—an Elder Conroy, from Buffalo—gave

Aaron the cold shoulder over his association with Elder Todd and made a pious production about having been completely unaware of the whole Post-it thing.

For his part, Aaron buried his head in his Bible and worked on his relationship with God. But privately he wondered if Jesus would have been so cruel to a boy who was just trying to have some harmless fun.

Setting the Date

Julie stepped out the front door, her turquoise yoga mat gripped in one hand. She stared out at the orange-rimmed horizon, yawned, stretched, and slipped on her shades. A little way into the courtyard she saw a young man sitting at the top of the steps that led down to the street. His tucked-in white dress shirt stretched up from the belt of his navy trousers and across his strong back. He appeared to be reading something. *That must be one of the missionaries,* she thought, slowly stepping up behind him. *Too bad Christian's not here—he could make a move.* It had been almost a week since they'd made the bet, and things were not looking good. The missionaries never seemed to be around. When they were, they stayed in pairs, always strapping on their helmets and heading out on 10-speeds. Christian hadn't even been able to start a conversation— let alone a flirtation—with any of them.

Julie moved closer. The missionary's hair was extremely short and neat, parted and pressed down, with a few fluffy wisps sticking up at the crown. From what she could see of his features, they were delicate and naive. In fact, he looked just like one of those old-time pioneer kids from *Little House on the Prairie*, a pretty little boy on his way to Sunday school.

Hell, I'd do him, she thought.

As she walked past him down the steps, she caught a glimpse of his Bible and wasn't surprised. What else would a missionary be reading? The Bible appeared to be peppered with an insane number of yellow sticky tabs. They looked like a row of carved pumpkin teeth.

Damn, what'd he do? Mark every page?

Julie went down the steps. She ran into Christian at the bottom.

"Hey, girl!" he said, his rippling body just begging to be adored in a thin, mustard-colored nylon jacket with cut-off sleeves. "Don't you look cute in your little velour sweatpants. Where're you off to?"

"Yoga," said Julie. She swept her eyes meaningfully toward the top of the steps. "You just getting back?"

"Yeah," said Christian, admiring his own flexed triceps. "Arm day." Then he glanced up, and when he saw what she had intended him to see—an opportunity to earn 50 bucks, have his tables bused, and his ego stroked—his own eyes widened.

"Ooh, nice muscle," said Julie. But her eyes said, *Come on, make a move.*

Nuh-uh, Christian telepathed back. *Too overt. Why don't you do something—come on, grease the wheels, baby.*

Julie turned, threw a quick smirk over her shoulder, and then went up the steps.

Aaron had kept his nose buried in his Bible through this exchange. Though expected to go door-to-door all day, he felt shy about initiating contact with his neighbors—especially after the beer incident. What if that guy had heard what Ryder said? It was just plain embarrassing.

As he skimmed the same phrase over and over—*I pray also that the eyes of your heart may be enlightened in order that you may know the hope to which he has called you*—he felt a light, sweet tap on his forearm. It felt amazing, as he hadn't felt a girl's touch since he left Pocatello and hugged his mom goodbye. It made him miss her even more. He looked at her. She was beautiful, with bright, kind eyes.

"Hey there." Her voice came out raspy—almost like a man's, but finer. "You know, I don't think we've met. I'm Julie Taylor." She stuck out her hand.

"Hi," said Aaron, shaking it. "I'm…Elder Davis."

"So, uh…whatcha reading?"

"I'm…just…studying, you know. Thought I'd come outside because…well, look at it."

Julie gazed out at the sunlit stucco bungalows with their potted cacti and bright-red bougainvillea. Palm fronds rustled over their heads. Birds posing as musical notes chirped from their places on telephone lines.

"Look at what?" she asked.

"I don't know, all this sun, I guess. These palm trees… And it's great just to be outside, you know, and feel warm without a coat. I'm from Idaho. It gets cold in October."

She frowned in sympathy. "Oh, bummer—well, it's pretty much like this all the time here." She cocked her head and called down to the sidewalk. "Isn't it, Christian?"

"Yeah."

Oh, thought Aaron. *His name is Christian. He was so proud of his beer offering yesterday, he forgot to introduce himself.*

"So," said Julie, determined to continue the conversation with the young missionary. "What is it you guys do?"

Aaron smiled. "We talk to people about our church."

"Oh, really?" said Julie. "Christian likes to talk to people."

Aaron glanced at him. "Sometimes it helps them find meaning in their lives."

"Isn't that interesting?" said Julie. She was laying it on thick.

Christian climbed halfway up the steps. Suddenly Aaron smelled him, his pit sweat, but also...*whoa!*...his other kind of sweat.

Christian said, "Yeah. That *is* interesting. Julie was just complaining the other day that her life is void of meaning."

"Void?" said Julie. "I said 'void'?"

"Mmm-hmm."

Aaron brightened. "Well, maybe we could come and talk with you."

"We would like that," said Julie.

"Tomorrow evening, maybe?"

"Mmm...Wednesday's better," she said.

"Yeah. Wednesday," said Christian.

"OK, Wednesday."

Aaron gave each of them a friendly but shy sort of smile. He shut his Bible, got up, and retreated to his bungalow, bounding through the open front door to share the good news with Ryder.

Christian and Julie watched him go.

"Bye," called Christian with forced significance. He turned to Julie. "Subtle."

"Yeah, well, I got 50 bucks riding on you."

"Yeah, well, don't worry, because that boy's as latent as they come."

"Are you serious?" Julie crowed.

"Shhh." Christian covered her mouth. He glanced over at the open door of the missionaries' bungalow. The coast was clear. He moved in close to her and whispered, "Sure I'm serious. You think I don't know a repressed homo when I see one? He holds his arms all tucked in against his body. He couldn't look me in the eye… His face turned seven shades of red—and trust me—I mean, you're hot and everything—but it wasn't you he was blushing over."

"Oh, my God, you're right."

"Honey," said Christian smugly. "You better figure out what you want to spend your money on, because once I get a chance to sit in the same room with this guy, there's no way we're losing this bet."

Christian and Traci sat at the bar, folding napkins in sullen silence. Could the world be any more unjust? Were the hateful always the ones to succeed? Just as they shared this thought, a pair of enemy thighs in a black leather miniskirt flounced across the floor behind them. Two giant bodyguards brought up the rear. Like synchronized machines, Traci and Christian's bar stools swiveled 45 degrees, and their narrowed eyes shot missiles at a platinum blond bull's-eye. Who did she think she was?

"Thank God," Traci whispered. "She's finally leaving."

Andrew reappeared from his crouched position behind the bar. Still as sentries, the trio kept all eyes trained on the door—until it shut.

Andrew leaned forward, polishing a shot glass. "Can you believe *Entertainment Weekly* called her 'the new sweetheart of American cinema'?"

"That cunt?" marveled Traci. "She made Julie take my table because she thought I hadn't bathed recently—like she should talk! Did you see her eat?"

"Yeah," said Andrew. "Did you check out her legs? Now I know why they call 'em calves."

Christian leaned in. "I bet after sex she smokes a ham."

Traci threw down her napkin and brayed with laughter. Suddenly Lila was there. She'd come sashaying up silently on her Stuart Weitzman heels. "Andrew, darling—a glass of that cuvée. And people"—she paused to adjust her glamorous black wrap—"I do hope we're not speaking disparagingly about one of our esteemed *clientele*. Gossip is so ignoble, especially regarding those less fortunate."

"Less fortunate?" fumed Traci through clenched teeth. "That cow?"

"Shhhhh." Christian placed a finger to his lips.

But Andrew was on to Lila's game. "You know something! C'mon...tell."

"Please, no." Lila placed her hand to her cleavage. "I would never tell tales such as...well, with the frequency she does it, the poor child must think that binging and purging are aerobic exercise."

The group gasped a collective "No!"

"Yes!" whispered Lila, casting her eyes from side to side. "And if I were a different sort, I'd suggest more of the purging, a little less of the binging."

Andrew placed her glass on the bar, and Christian

lifted it. "Here, here," he toasted. Then he passed it to his boss.

"Thank you, dearest. But," she added, "I would never say such things—for gossip is the lowest form of discourse. Children, you should avoid it...if at all possible."

Christian noticed something frail in his boss's eyes. He studied her face. "Are you OK?"

"Certainly. Never better." She held her glass aloft, and then downed a small gulp. "I'll be in the office cooking the books, if I am needed."

As she moved off, Andrew remembered something. "Oh! You got another call from Ben."

Lila waved off the news, pushing her way through the swinging double doors.

"He sounded kind of insistent," Andrew shouted after her—but he was too late. Lila had already disappeared.

"Do you suppose," Traci asked, "Lila is hiding a boyfriend from us?"

"Didn't you listen?" said Christian. "Gossip is the lowest form of discourse."

"Oh, please."

Just then Julie skulked up to the bar register to ring up her last receipts. Having just spent the last part of the evening being pleasant to a woman she couldn't stand, she looked whipped and haggard. Even pulled back, her braids were drooping. "Aargh!" she screamed suddenly, and kicked the counter. "That fucking skank! That's not a tip—that's an indictment."

"Whoa, whoa," said Traci. "Take it down, Julie. Christ, who pissed in your Cheerios?"

"Who else," asked Andrew, "if not the new cheapskate of American cinema?"

"No," said Julie. "It's not just the tip. I'm under a lot of stress."

Christian put his arm around her. "Who's messing with my girl? Just tell me. Huh? Is it that new A&R guy?"

Julie rolled her eyes and nodded.

"Who's that?" said Andrew. "A new boyfriend?"

"She has drinks with him," Christian explained, "so he'll listen to her demo, and now she fears for her virtue. He's actually kind of cute"—he pulled his beefy arm from around her and cracked his knuckles—"so if you want me to talk to him…"

"C'mon, I bust my ass making a great demo, and now I can't get anyone to listen to it. And this guy? So obvious he only wanted to fuck me."

"Poor baby," cooed Traci. "I thought he was cute too."

Julie looked at her. "You'd have sex to help your career?"

Traci nodded. "I left New York—what's a little sex?"

"Honey," said Andrew, "I've blown a guy just so he'd leave my apartment. Sex for my career would be noble. And speaking of a career in sex…Christian, how are things coming with that little sacred panty raid?"

Julie perked up. "We're having them over Wednesday night."

"Who?" gasped Traci.

"The Mormon boys."

"No!"

"Yes!"

"What for?"

Christian grinned. "Spin the bottle, if I play my cards right."

Lila Montagne was a walking portrait of glamour and poise. These qualities evaporated when she entered her office. Her massive teak desk, an import from Bali, was cluttered with knickknacks, tax forms, receipts, and unopened junk mail. The walls of the small 10-by-12-foot chamber were covered with a hodgepodge of travel and film set souvenirs, of lopsidedly draped red-and-gold tapestries, dusty framed black-and-white stills. Here she could let herself go, let Lila be Lila. And so she was now, as she hunched over her desk and chewed on a plastic paperclip, the receiver of an antique dial-faced phone pressed to her ear.

"Ben, I have thought about it!"

Her bifocal-covered eyes drifted over to a large framed photo on the wall, where a sultry, gorgeous, and much younger incarnation of herself stood with one arm strung casually over the shoulder of a striking man in a director's chair.

"But I'm not ready to make that kind of decision yet."

Her attention was distracted by Christian in the doorway.

Christian had frozen there, shocked to see his boss looking less like an elegant, aging diva of the screen and more like an exhausted gambling bookie. He knew his boss was a secret slob, but he had never seen her slouch—she looked almost masculine.

"I have to go now. OK, I'll call you back." *Cling*. Lila hung up, sat up, slid down her bifocals, and peered at her worst—but by far her favorite—employee.

Christian came forward with a small slip of paper in his hand. "Here's Andrew's wine order."

"Thank you," said Lila.

He placed it in front of her, then turned to leave. At the doorway, he hesitated.

"Yes? Was there something else?"

Christian took a timid step toward her. "Everybody's saying this Ben guy is your secret boyfriend. But he's not. He's a doctor—isn't he?" Christian paused to gauge her reaction, but she just stared blankly back at him. "Is everything…I mean, are you OK?"

Lila wore a mask of cool. "Young man, I will not be the subject of gossip in my own establishment. Do you understand me?"

"Yes. Sorry." He left, slinking off like a bad puppy.

Lila watched him go, took a sip of wine, pushed up her bifocals, and began shuffling papers. She cast her wide, bleary eyes up at the photo and sighed. "You were always difficult, Henry, but this—*this* absolutely takes the cake."

Traci

Traci Levine had been in Los Angeles now for just a little over three years. Her hopes had been high at first. She had majored in drama at Vassar after taking an acting class her sophomore year. She loved acting, working on set design, and lighting, but best of all, the camaraderie that came from working with a good group of people and completing a project together. In her senior year, she'd had several starring roles, including Hedda in *Hedda Gabler* and Grace in *To Sir With Love*. These successes gave her the confidence to move to New York City to pursue an acting career. Besides, all her friends were moving there.

Her parents, who lived in Great Neck, Long Island, weren't particularly happy about that decision; her dad, a podiatrist, had for some undisclosed reason hoped she would eventually enter the Foreign Service. When Traci had been in the city for two months and only gotten one audition for an off-off-Broadway production of Tennessee Williams's *Night of the Iguana* and a minor part in an even more minor commercial, her father informed her that if she did not reconsider, he was going to cut her off.

The conversation had been a tough one. Her dad had come into the city for an appointment with his accountant, and she'd met him for lunch immediately afterward.

"Guess what, Dad, I have a spot in a commercial. I'm going to be on TV!"

"Oh, really?" He seemed interested. "That's great. What kind of commercial? Hair? Car?"

"It's for insect repellent. For a new brand, actually… called Keep Away…" She watched her dad's face fall.

"Insect repellent? Keep Away? I've never even heard of that!"

"That's because it's new, Dad," Traci said quickly. "But market research has shown that it's going to be big…"

He interrupted her. "How big can bug repellent get?"

"Seriously, Dad. This is a great opportunity. It's the first commercial they're doing and…well, you've heard of West Nile Virus, haven't you?"

"How much does it pay?" He bit angrily into his club sandwich.

"Well, it pays $1,000—but there could be royalties. I know someone who got rich off nothing but commercial royalties. So even if it isn't much, it could, you know, lead to…"

Dr. Levine put his sandwich down and leaned back in his chair. "Traci…" he began heavily, "it's been two months already, and this is the first real job you've been offered, isn't it?"

"But…"

He held up his hand. "Let me finish, Traci. A thousand dollars isn't going to last you a week in this city. Listen, your mother and I have been talking, and we're not sure we can afford to support you much longer, while you flounder about, trying to become an actress. Do you even *know* how competitive it is?"

Traci sighed. "Dad, I am not fucking floundering!" Her voice rose and carried across the restaurant. "I mean, it takes a long time. I can't suddenly become successful overnight. But I'm starting to make some contacts, and if you and Mom will just give me a chance, then…"

Dr. Levine interrupted her again. "Your mother and I will make sure you have enough to last through the end of this month. We paid for four years of Vassar, which—let me remind you—is *not* the cheapest school around. And we were happy to do it. But this is it, Traci. This isn't playing around anymore. You need to take responsibility for what your mother and I, quite frankly, find to be a questionable career choice."

Traci's limbs felt icy. " 'Questionable career choice'? Dad, being an actor is perfectly respectable. Just because I don't want to be the next ambassador to the United Nations is no reason to accuse me of being involved in something questionable."

Dr. Levine took a sip of his Sprite and looked thoughtful. "Well, there's something to be said for a career in the Foreign Service. It's solid. It's dependable, and it's interesting."

"Maybe to you it's interesting," Traci pouted. "But to me. Well. It isn't."

"Why don't you consider giving it a try? Your mother and I have talked this over, and we've agreed that if you're interested, we'll pay for you to take Mandarin Chinese at City College. Now, that's a language that'll really get you somewhere! In only a few years, China's going to be the biggest market in the world…"

Traci clenched her teeth. "I'm…not…interested! Besides, I hate Chinese food. I love acting. I'm passionate about it, and that's what I'm going to do."

Her father looked displeased. "Well, your mother and I thought you might be grateful for such an opportunity. But clearly we were wrong." He dropped his fork loudly on the table. "Anyway, Traci. The bottom line is, if you want to be an *actress*"—he pronounced it as if it were a dirty word—"you're on your own at the end of the month. And if you succeed at it, well…we'll be the first to congratulate you. Good luck." He signaled for the check.

Her dad had been right, though. That first commercial hadn't led to the plethora of job offers Traci had expected. She collected her thousand dollars from the bug repellent folks and—based on the advice of a friend who insisted that Hollywood was the place to be—spent a good part of it on a one-way ticket to Los Angeles.

She was down to her last 10 bucks when one day, as she walked dejectedly along after a failed audition, she spotted a HELP WANTED sign in a restaurant called Lila's. It was like a miracle: She walked in, secured the job, and hadn't looked back since.

First Date

Christian and Julie had decorated their apartment in expectation of the day *Architectural Digest* would run a piece on rent-controlled units in Hollywood. They'd joyfully painted each tiny room a warm color, with the sills and trim powder-painted white. There were accent walls. Pop-culture collectibles—like the talking *Planet of the Apes* doll propped up next to the toaster—contributed to a sense of irony and playfulness. An antique chair or bureau here and there acted as foils to their cheap Ikea furniture. Plant life was in abundance.

Julie sat cross-legged in her socks. Christian sat with his knees apart in his flip-flops. Both wore bright-colored T-shirts, faded jeans, and slack-jawed expressions as they lounged on the sofa, gaping at the two young men in bleached-white shirts and navy-blue ties sitting across from them on a pair of knockoff Eames chairs. Elder Davis, the cute blond missionary they'd talked to at the top of the steps, held a flip album of religious pictures at the end of his knees, and he was going on and on about some guy name Joseph Smith and some golden tablets that came down from heaven.

Christian twirled and tugged at a lock of his hair. He seemed mesmerized by Aaron's words but was actually fixated on his soft lips—as well as giving him a makeover in his mind's eye. *Eyebrows need waxing, definitely lose the tie…*

Julie nudged him. He swayed gently. She nudged him harder.

"What? Oh…"

Aaron's face was all shiny sincerity. His brows lifted slightly. His eyes glistened. "…and that's how, through Joseph Smith, God restored the true Church of Jesus Christ to the Earth." He paused lovingly on the final picture in the book: a portrait of a very worried-looking Jesus Christ. "Any questions?"

Christian raised his hand. The pit of his yellow T-shirt was a tiny bit damp. "I have one," he said. "How come if God talks to Joseph Smith, Smith gets to be a prophet, but if God talks to me, I'm schizophrenic?"

Ryder squinted with annoyance, but took a stab at it. "Well, he was sort of special…"

"And how does your church feel about black people?" asked Julie.

"That's a good question." Aaron glanced at Ryder. "African-American members have been allowed to hold the priesthood since 1978."

"*Allowed?*" Julie crossed her arms.

"Since disco," said Christian. "That's progressive."

"What about women?" added Julie.

"Yeah," said Christian. "When did women get to be priests?"

Ryder met his eyes uncomfortably. "Women don't hold the priesthood. What women get is to be wives and to be mothers and to share in its blessings."

"See, Julie?" said Christian as he patted her knee. "Sharing. Sharing is good."

Julie shot him a look, then with complete deadpan delivery: "Christian was wondering what your church's stand is on gay rights."

The entire room froze. Molecules halted in their tracks. Airborne dust particles abandoned their trajectories.

Aaron coughed to clear his throat. "Well," he said. "Um…"

"No such thing as gay rights," Elder Ryder said. " 'Gay' and 'right' don't even belong in the same sentence."

Christian leaned forward. "Oh, but then let me guess, 'right' and 'right wing' go hand in hand!"

Elder Ryder stared hard at him. "Yeah. God hates homos."

The air in the room felt stuffy and surreal. All the tiny sounds in it were accentuated: the tick of a Mickey Mouse wall clock, the refrigerator's electric thrum, a creak as Julie shifted a bit on the sofa… Someone swallowed.

Suddenly Christian came to his feet. He leaned in and stabbed a finger at Ryder's chest. "You're gonna come into my home and tell me God hates homosexuals…?"

"…and the French," piped in Aaron.

Ryder turned his head. "God hates the French?"

Christian straightened up and put both hands on his hips.

Aaron shrugged. "Everyone hates the French."

Christian smiled.

Julie laughed out loud.

Mormons proselytize in pairs. Why? So the misguided

can't toy with them. When Elder Ryder had still been a greenie, a perfectly interested and intelligent-seeming Venezuelan woman had invited him in with his proselytizing companion and served them each a cup of herbal tea with a plateful of cookies, only to start firing off statistics about the so-called racism and misogyny of the church. She'd turned out to be some kind of radical professor—women's studies, he was sure she had called it, whatever that was. Sometimes, still, her tense, angry lips and furrowed eyebrows visited Ryder in his nightmares. Then there was that old retired fellow, who'd gotten up slowly and hobbled out of the room—then came back holding a sawed-off shotgun. "So, you telling me, you rewrote the Bible?" he'd roared, cocking his rifle like a geriatric Rambo. "You get your self-righteous asses outta here!"

Ryder had recounted these worst-case scenarios to Aaron before they even went out on their first cold-call. "The principle being," he'd told him, "the whole purpose of the buddy system is so one guy can watch the other guy's back."

Well, Aaron had failed to watch Ryder's back. And now, as he fumbled through the refrigerator for the milk, he heard the disappointment in Ryder's voice:

"My mother was French."

Aaron straightened up, closed the fridge, and with his free hand opened the cupboard to get a glass. "That explains a lot."

Ryder's face turned red.

"You know," said Aaron, filling his glass, "that was

totally out of line, what you said in there—that God hates…homosexuals. God doesn't hate anybody."

"Oh, please, get off it," said Ryder. "You know what your problem is?"

Aaron plunked his milk carton down. "What?"

"You're all, like…oh, everybody's a child of God, and all that bullpucky. Part of why we're out here, son…we're supposed to call the wicked to repentance."

"We get to decide who's wicked?"

"The decision's already made. I mean, we're over there and they start in being all ignorant and stuff, tossing around all that 'How does your church feel about black people?' and 'How does your church feel about women?' and all of that faggot stuff. Think they weren't baiting us? Think they didn't have an agenda? Well, guess again, Greenie. That's why I'm the senior missionary here." Ryder paced the kitchen. "And her, for all we know she could be one of them, you know"—he lowered his voice to a whisper—"Ellen-lovers."

Aaron leaned against the counter. "Someone who likes comedy?"

Ryder rolled his eyes. "A les-bee-yun. Don't act like such a 'tard. You know Sodom and Gomorrah had nothing on this place—and you want to ease up on people."

"Judge not that ye be not judged."

"And that's what to me?" Ryder grabbed the carton and drank from it.

"That would be Jesus. It's in the *Bible*."

"Yeah? Well, how about 'Whosoever transgress against me, him shall you judge'? It's the flippin' *Book of Mormon*!"

"Wow," Aaron said, looking around the room. "He actually knows a scripture."

Ryder wiped his chin. "Yeah," he said. "I know one or two. You know, you come here over from Pocatello, this stake president's kid, and you're all hot snot, just because you can quote your sticks. But don't act like I'm some dumb over-homer. You're no better than I am, and you're no better than any of these freaks in this freaking city." Ryder was panting when he finished.

"None of us are," said Aaron. "That's what I'm saying."

"Oh, shut up."

Having just jokingly restored the sanctity of their living room through a quick sage-burning ritual, Julie handed Christian a beer. "So," she said, taking a seat in the chair across from him. "Was that totally bizarre, or what?"

"That was *totally* bizarre," said Christian. "I thought Mormons were supposed to be nice, you know, like shiny-happy robots for God. But that Ryder guy, whoo! Angry Man. Hey, and what's with that whole 'elder' thing? Don't these guys even have first names?"

"I know!" she laughed. "What are they, like, 18? And they walk around dressed like these middle-age corporate sales reps."

"Wanna know who they dress like?" said Christian.

"Who?" said Julie.

"Us—in our stupid work clothes."

"Oh, my God. Now I really feel sorry for them."

Christian drained the rest of his beer. "You know," he

said, tugging at the back of his hair, "I still think the blond one's cute."

"Cute?" asked Julie. "I thought you said latent."

"Oh, yeah," said Christian smiling. "Cute, latent…"

"Are you sure he's latent?"

Christian looked at her. "Oh, yeah."

"What if it's just a Mormon thing?"

"Believe me, I know what I'm talking about."

"He is cute," said Julie. She sighed. "So earnest."

Christian stretched out catlike on the sofa. "Yeah… You won't catch me chasing after Angry Man."

"I hear that. What a jerk."

Christian winked and added slyly, "But I did think maybe you kind of liked him a little…"

"Oh, yeah, right."

"I'm serious. I sensed an intense vibe between you two."

Julie ran over and tried to smother Christian with one of the furry blue sofa cushions. "That's disgusting. Since when have I been attracted to uptight pencil-neck white boys?"

"Come on, girl," Christian teased. "Maybe you need to branch out. I mean, he obviously had one on for you."

"Shut up!"

"OK, stop that—OK, OK—I was only joking. All I'm saying is that in his sick chauvinistic mind, you're probably the ultimate temptress. You pushed his buttons, baby."

Julie thought this over. "You're gross." She swung the pillow at him.

"Just keep in mind that behind those Kmart trousers— balls of a tiger, baby."

That night Christian dreamed of a dark hotel room, and of a pale, blond missionary in shimmering garments that clung to his body like liquid silver. He reached out to Christian in terror as he drifted back toward a furious stark-white blizzard. Christian extended his hand, but as he did so, the missionary's garments seemed to stretch up, out, and around him, encapsulating him in a giant cocoon. "Wait!" Christian screamed as the cocoon turned into a ball of light that drifted up, shrank to an intense white dot, and slowly disappeared.

Second Date

Nintendo is not just a game for kids. Adolescents can play it too.

Christian sat on the floor, slouched against the couch in a tight red tank top and black sweats, his legs apart, his joystick between them. His thumbs flew at warp speed. His eyes darted all over the TV screen.

Suddenly a shadow flashed across the drawn linen curtains.

Was that...?

Christian dropped his game, scrambled up, and ran to the window. Cautiously, he pulled aside the curtain with one finger and peeked through the wooden Levelor blinds just in time to catch a view of that cute blond missionary hustling across the courtyard. He watched his neighbor's butt flex cheek to cheek, disappearing down the steps to the laundry room as its owner struggled to maintain control of a flimsy beige plastic laundry tub and a giant bottle of liquid detergent.

Christian was practically licking his chops. *Finally*, he thought, *a chance to be alone with him.* It didn't take long for the experienced seducer, his arms moving faster than his thumbs had on his game pad, to gather up a meager load of colors, toss everything into a compact turquoise laundry basket, and sprint with it out the door.

But when he entered the laundry room, he was surprised to find the poor missionary bent over a washing machine with his head on his arms. Was he crying? If so, he probably didn't need company. But before Christian could turn and leave, the screen door slammed shut behind him.

Aaron straightened up, saw Christian, and—despite his red-rimmed eyes—made an effort to look casual. He grabbed a pair of Levi's and stuffed them into the washer.

Christian stepped forward. "Are you OK?"

Aaron pretended to read the dial on the machine. "Um, yeah. I'm fine."

Christian set down his laundry basket. "Ring around the collar. I completely understand."

"What? Oh…" Aaron forced a smile. "No, really, it's nothing."

"Look," said Christian. "If there's a problem, maybe I could come back later…?"

Aaron faced him. He threw out his hands. "Maybe I'm just homesick, OK?"

"Homesick?" said Christian. "For *Idaho*?"

Aaron winced. "OK," he said, laughing. "Fine."

Christian dropped a few pairs of bikini briefs into the washer. "Sorry. That came out wrong. You know, it's just…well, when I left home, zoom, like a rocket. But if…" He paused, realizing something. "You've never been away from home before, have you?"

"What?" said Aaron. "No—I've been away from home, just not for two whole years."

"Could be worse," quipped Christian in a thick British accent. "Could be rainin.'"

Aaron looked confused, but a few moments later it dawned on him. "Hey, I know what that's from. That's from *Young Frankenstein.* 'Why, thank you, doctor.'"

They shared a bashful smile.

"So," said Christian. "Two years, huh?"

"Yeah, I know—sounds crazy, doesn't it?" said Aaron. "We're not allowed to call or go home for holidays. They can't visit."

"Wow," said Christian. "Where do I sign up?"

"Hey, I happen to like my family…." Aaron stared vacantly into space. "After all, a boy's best friend is his mother."

Christian watched him, feeling a little freaked. The kid was weirder than he thought. What kind of cult was this? Unless… "Wait! Uh…*Psycho*! That's from *Psycho*, right?" His face went slack. "'She just goes a bit mad sometimes. We all go a bit mad sometimes.'"

Aaron laughed, then he lowered his eyes. He felt discombobulated—curious, attracted, confused…

"Hey, it can't be so bad," said Christian. "At least you have your friends here, right?"

Aaron wrinkled his nose. "Who? Ryder? Nah, I barely even know the guy. We just got assigned to each other a couple of weeks ago."

"Oh. Well, better you than me."

There was another awkward moment. Christian finished tossing his clothes in.

"What do you mean 'assigned'?"

"Every missionary gets assigned a companion. We're roommates. We go out tracting together."

"Tracting?"

"That's what we call 'proselytizing'—spreading the good word about our church. You know, like door-to-door salesmen…"

"And you don't even like the guy?"

Aaron shrugged. "Not much I can do about it."

Christian paused with his quarters in hand. "Stuck with a guy you don't even like, cut off from your family. Isn't that a harsh exile, for a church mostly about family?"

"Who am I to say? 'Neither be ye of a doubtful mind.'"

"Hmm. Uh…that's, uh…that's from a Merchant/Ivory movie, right?"

"No," said Aaron. "That's actually from the Bible."

"Oh, right. I figured it was either that or *Weekend at Bernie's*." Christian plugged in his quarters. "Kind of a funny coincidence," he added slyly, "that all you guys are named Elmer, huh?"

Aaron staggered back, laughing incredulously. "Elmer? You think I'm an Elmer?"

"What? You're not?"

"No. It's not Elmer, doofus. It's *Elder*. It's a title." He stuffed in a pair of khakis. "Elder, you know—like an elder of the church."

"Ohhh," said Christian. "Good thing. Because naming you Elmer, that's just mean."

"Yeah," said Aaron. "Hey, but you knew I wasn't named Elmer. It was on our badges all night the other night."

"Psych!" Christian slapped Aaron's shoulder with the

back of his hand. "Maybe. But you still fell for it. So what *is* your first name anyway?"

"Uh...we're not allowed to use it."

"What? Why not?"

Aaron looked at him. "We're not allowed to do a lot of things."

Christian searched his face. There was so much there, yet he seemed so...trapped.

"Aaron. It's"—a meaningful glance—"Aaron."

"Aaron," said Christian. "I like that."

Aaron gestured with his palm up. "Now I'm supposed to smite you to death, with a plowshare or something. But I won't tell if you won't."

Christian leaned over Aaron's laundry pile. "Uh...you're gonna sort those, right?" He reached over and began to sift through it. "See, colors and whites don't mix, Aaron." He pulled the bottom half of a set of long johns from the pile, but before he could get a good look, Aaron snatched them away.

"Yeah, OK," Aaron said. "Thanks, I think I get it."

Christian backed off. "Oh, wait. You've never done your own laundry before either, have you?"

"Maybe," said Aaron. "But maybe I'm just not used to doing *everybody's,* OK? But that's what I have to do, because I'm the greenie."

Christian cocked his head. "The what?"

"The greenie," said Aaron. "The new guy, so I have to do everybody's laundry." He paused. "You know, in accordance with prophecy."

"Really?"

Trying to keep from laughing, Aaron started up the washer. He turned and threw a playful punch at Christian. "Psych!"

Christian crossed his eyes. "Ha ha ha."

An easy, amiable laugh flushed the sadness from Aaron's face. Christian joined in. They were having a good time.

"Dude," said Aaron, staring into Christian's eyes. "You're too easy."

Christian maintained eye contact and stepped into Aaron's space. They were almost nose to nose. His voice dropped a notch. "So I've been told."

Aaron held his ground for a long uncertain moment. He felt cornered, cornered by 225 pounds of pure primal sexuality in the form of a grown-up Mowgli from *The Jungle Book*—a gay Mowgli, with gelled hair and designer jeans. What did this mean? Where was it going? It was powerful, it was frightening...

It was wrong.

Aaron broke away. Snatching up his laundry basket, he slid his back along the wall. "Um, well, thanks for, you know, the wash tips and...and everything." As he eased out of the room, it took all the self-control he had not to openly bolt.

Smack, smack, smack, smack. Christian listened to Aaron's feet hit the steps.

Twelve steps, four smacks, he mused happily, gathering stray wads of lint from the top of the dryer. *He must've taken those babies three at a time.*

Sacred Hoops

Sunlight flooded in through the window above the kitchen sink, glinting off the Spanish tile counter as the yellow-gloved Harmon scrubbed it with a Brillo pad. Brushing the last of the crumbs into the drain, he aimed the faucet over the garbage disposal and flipped a switch. *Dink! Dink! Dink! Dink!* The sound made Harmon's heart skip. He quickly hit the switch, turned off the water, and reached into the disposal. A badly dinged-up spoon came out, pinched between his fingers. "Ah, crap...oops." He glanced into the living room to see if Davis had heard him, but all he saw was the back of the new kid's head.

What? thought Harmon. *He's still folding laundry? What's up with him?*

Harmon tiptoed over to the sofa where the yellow-haired neophyte clutched a pair of long johns, hands poised, about to fold. Harmon watched him. Nothing was happening. He'd seen this kind of behavior before, especially with the greenies. What Davis needed was a good cheering up. He crept up behind him, and—with the theme from the movie *Jaws* playing in his head—extended his gloved hand toward the back of Aaron's head. He swam it back and forth for a moment.

Suddenly his hand curled up and his sudsy finger

darted forward. Aaron jumped out of his socks. His legs and arms jerked out like he was having a seizure. Harmon kept his focus and wormed deeper into his ear, going for broke.

"Aaaah!" Aaron swatted Harmon's hand away. "Jeez, Elder!"

"Gotcha!" Harmon laughed, sliding off his gloves. "Oh, man, that had to be one of the best wet willies ever. The execution was perfect. I give myself a '10.'" He sat at the edge of the sofa and draped a brotherly arm across Aaron's shoulder. "You were about a thousand miles away over here," he said chuckling.

Aaron tried to ignore him.

Harmon lowered his face to look into Aaron's eyes. "How're you doing, Green?" He began to rhythmically massage the top of Aaron's arm. "Everything OK?"

"Sure. Fine," said Aaron. He hurried to squirm free and moved to the other end of the sofa. Harmon sat cross-legged where Aaron had been sitting and picked up a pair of underwear from the basket on the floor. "You sure, Green?"

Aaron met his eyes briefly. "Yeah," he said. "I'm sure."

Harmon continued to help Aaron fold. "You know," he said. "When I was a greenie, it was really tough. I used to pray I'd die during the night so I wouldn't have to wake up to another day of this."

Aaron looked at him. "You're joking me, right?"

"Nah," answered Harmon, pausing to reflect awhile. "Oh, my heck, I was wracked. Jennifer would write me these 'Oh, baby, I'm not sure I can wait' letters… It was hard-core."

"Wow!" Aaron laughed.

"Oh, yeah." Harmon scratched at his groin. "I thought of baggin' it, but there's no way I'd be able to face up to going home. You know, the family, Salt Lake…" He frowned, picking up a shirt, then dropping it. "I mean, I had two of the General Authorities at my missionary farewell. You've got to know what that's like. Your dad's a stake president, right?"

Aaron nodded.

"So you must know as well as I do, that it's all about knowing how to play the game. You learn the hoops you're expected to jump through and then jump through them."

Aaron nodded again, but he couldn't believe what he was hearing. Jumping through the right hoops…is that what this was all about?

Harmon leaned across the sofa to tap him lightly on the arm. "Come on, Green, think about it. They set this thing up to be difficult, OK? We can't listen to music. We can't watch movies. We can't use computers. We can't swim. We're never supposed to be alone. I mean, come on, we're 19…20 years old and we're not even allowed to beat off." He grabbed Aaron's wrist. "I'm serious. Some nights I wake up and I find teeth marks on my headboard. Go ahead and laugh. But look, I put my time in here, so that I can go home, so that I can marry Jennifer, so that I can finally nail her." He dropped Aaron's wrist and slouched back against the sofa, lost suddenly in his own daydream. His head swung back and forth. "It's amazing what we'll do for sex."

Aaron leaned in. "And that's it? Don't you ever wonder?"

Harmon looked up. "Don't I ever wonder what?"

"Don't you ever wonder...what else? I mean, don't you ever think about other girls, you know, maybe..."—he searched Harmon's face—"other kinds of stuff."

Harmon narrowed his eyes. "Everybody thinks of 'stuff,' Elder." He picked up his gloves and stood up. "But you just learn to put it out of your head."

Christian and Julie loved playing hoops. Sometimes they'd drive to the Hollywood Y and play full-court, shocking the guys who thought Julie couldn't run with them—she could. Sometimes they'd drive over to Plummer Park, or pick up a game at the high school on Fairfax. But more often lately—especially when they were feeling a little lazy, or on weekdays—they'd just walk down the street to the old clay half-court at the local playground.

That Monday afternoon, after a few half-assed games of HORSE during which much gossip was exchanged, they decided to play one-on-one.

Julie took the ball at the top of the key. Damp spots of sweat showed through her sleeveless, cut-off T-shirt. She swung the ball below her knees and stared at the basket, then at Christian. "What do we have? Six to three?" She jab-stepped a few times. He didn't go for it.

"That'd be three to six... *my lead.*"

Julie dribbled right, but Christian read it perfectly and sidestepped. Poking the ball loose with his long arm, he came up with it. "Oh, ho, ho, look at this!" he taunted. He high-bounced the ball, laughing when Aaron and Ryder walked onto the court in drawstring sweatpants and loose gray T-shirts.

Christian looked them over. Ryder had a basketball under his arm and was walking over like some kind of hotshot. Christian's eyes met Aaron's. "Hey, Elder."

"Excuse me," said Ryder, his chin jutting upward. "We'd like to play here."

"OK…" said Christian. "But we're *already* playing here."

Ryder slapped his ball. "You're just fartin' around."

"How vivid," said Julie. "We're playing, see? Show him, Christian."

Christian dribbled with an intentional lack of coordination. "Bounce the ball. Bounce the ball." He bounced-passed it awkwardly to Julie

"Bounce the ball," said Julie, bouncing it back to him.

"Bounce the ball." Christian bounced it back.

Aaron grabbed Ryder's sleeve. "C'mon, let's just go."

Ryder wrenched his arm away, and turned to Christian. "No, no way. You're just jerking us around, man. There's only one afternoon a week when I can be normal and shoot some hoops, and you have to go and get all ignorant about it."

Christian spun away from Ryder and broke into a Shaquille O'Neal body-wiggling dance he was sure would provoke the shit out of him. "Will you listen to that, Julie? And I didn't think Mormons liked *whine*…"

"I didn't know fairies liked sports."

"Fairies?" Christian stopped dancing and tucked the ball under his arm. "How seventh-grade. But then…"

Julie snatched the ball from Christian and posed with it on her hip. "Why don't we play two-on-two?"

Ryder looked flustered. He pursed his lips. "But you're…"

"I'm a girl? So I can't play? But then again, I am black, so maybe I can. Your problem's gonna be deciding which one of your narrow-minded stereotypes is gonna kick your lily-white ass."

"Yeah, right."

"Afraid you'll get beat?" taunted Julie.

"By a *girl*," added Christian. "And a faaaag?"

Aaron stood by with his arms folded. "This is stupid," he interjected. "Let them have the court."

"No way, Elder." Ryder jabbed his finger in Julie's face. "We'll mop you two like a dirty floor."

Julie bent and rolled her ball to the fence. "We'll use your ball," she said. "So you won't be able to use it as an excuse."

"That's fine," said Ryder. "'Cause you'll be the ones needing an excuse." He took one dribble and drained an easy jumper.

"Ooh," said Christian. "I'm scared."

"Shut up and let's play." Ryder grabbed his ball out of the net and dribbled out for a three-pointer. Now that all the preliminary trash talk had been gotten out of the way, he was warming up like it was the NBA Finals. He circled the ball between his knees, behind his back…

"I thought you wanted to play," said Christian.

"One more layup."

"Whatever," said Julie. "We're shirts. You're skins."

Aaron pulled down the hem of his T-shirt and blushed. "Uh...no."

"Fine," said Christian. "We'll be skins." He and Julie peeled off their shirts.

"Whoa!" Ryder's head whipped around at the arrival of Julie's incredible breasts, which lit up the court like a neon sign in her blue semi-sheer sports bra. *Bonk.* He ran straight into the pole under the basket and went down. He lay on his back, holding his forehead. "Ow."

Aaron tried to keep from laughing. "That wasn't fair," he said to Julie. "Just...put your shirt on. We'll keep it straight."

"Shoot for outs?" said Ryder.

"Whatever." Christian tucked his shirt into the back pocket of his sweats. "Just take it."

Ryder held the ball at the top of the key. He passed it to Aaron, who bounced it right back to him as he took a slippery cut to the hoop. It looked like an easy layup, but—blam!—Christian came flying from out of nowhere and blocked his shot right into the fence.

"Uh-uh," he taunted. "Not in my house, sister."

Eight baskets later, with an even score, the game was getting physical. Christian dribbled the ball while Aaron guarded him closely, bumping him hard as he reached in. "You reach," said Christian. "I teach." He flipped a no-look pass to Julie at the top of the key. Julie faked and sent Ryder into the air. As he was on his way down, she was on her way up for a fall-away jumper than got nothing but net.

Julie pumped her fist like Jordan. "Oh, yeah. Oh,

yeah." She high-fived Christian, and they shouted in unison: "Girl powah!"

"Yeah, baby," said Christian. "You put him in the popcorn machine."

Two plays later, Ryder had the ball at the top of the key. "Post up on him!" he shouted at Aaron. "Post up—you can score all day."

Aaron and Christian muscled each other around under the basket. "You can play," said Aaron.

Christian shoved him off balance. "That's just one of my skills," he murmured into his ear. Aaron shivered. Christian shoved him with a forearm, then leaned into him hard from behind, jamming his crotch against Aaron's tailbone. "I played in high school…found out all the hot jocks were 'doing it,' but only with other jocks."

The mental image was too much for Aaron. Ryder threw him the ball and it bounced off his chest. Christian picked it up and went in for the easy bucket.

"Hey," said Aaron crossly. "Let's cut the chatter, OK? Let's just play."

"We could," said Julie. "If that wasn't game."

Divine Intervention

One wall of the young missionary elders' living room was taken up by a 4-by-6-foot block of yellow laminate-paper thumb-tacked into place. A giant calendar grid had been hand-drawn on it using a yardstick and a purple Sharpie marker pen, and inside each box was a list of the proselytizers' appointments. Once a family decided they wanted to learn more about the church, the two missionary companions—one senior and one junior—would set up a series of six home appointments, during each of which a prescribed group of lessons, or "discussions" would be presented. The missionaries were usually up at 6 A.M., and after a period of group and individual prayer, they left the bungalow at 9 for their appointments. Some of the appointments they had gotten for themselves, but many were assigned to them by the mission office.

When they didn't have appointments, the missionaries were tracting—in other words, proselytizing on cold calls so they could set up more appointments. The primary goal of the missionary was to spread the truth of the church, but he also hoped to put up numbers—to bring in as many converts as he could.

For Aaron and Ryder, the big yellow chart showed a second appointment with the Ramos family in Echo

Park—scheduled for the following morning at 7 A.M. so the man of the house (a janitor who worked double shifts) could be there. Ryder hated these morning appointments. He was not what you'd call a "morning person," he'd told Aaron, after which Aaron had wondered if there was any time of day when Ryder *was* a person, because he hadn't noticed him being an afternoon or evening person either—and at night he was always sound asleep.

Strips of hazy late-afternoon light cut through the blinds, striping the thighs of Elder Ryder's jeans while he snoozed audibly from the puce sofa. His Bible was open facedown over his chest. His left arm was tucked behind the throw pillow that pushed up his head. His socks, which were slipping off his toes like little elf caps, emitted a faint odor.

On the floor in front of him, behind a pushed-out, cluttered coffee table, Harmon and Gilford sprawled with their feet pointing opposite directions in adjacent bean-bag chairs. Their Bibles were open face-up on their laps. And the backs of their heads rested against each other as they reviewed the designated scriptures.

On the other side of Harmon, Aaron sat in a hard wooden chair with his elbows on his knees and his spine curled into a *C*, forcing his nose as far into his Bible as possible. The physical contact between Harmon and Gilford made him feel tense and sweaty. He kept his eyes averted from the fact of Harmon's dark but fine brown hair mixing with Gilford's stiff bottlebrush of blond. One look had already given him a queasy sexual rush.

Aaron had always felt a bit of anxiety around the easy

physical affection between other men. But his discomfort had escalated since he'd run into Christian in the laundry room, and then on the basketball court the other day. The incidents had thrown him into a constant state of enhanced sensuality. Everything he touched seemed to radiate through him. Even the Bible he held in his hands, the smell of its pages, the feel of the leather in his hands was somehow seductive. Something was going on between them. He knew it. What he didn't know was if the other elders could tell. Aaron was petrified of their disgust.

Harmon chuckled as he scanned the room and compared his ragtag crew to Jesus' apostles. He was fond of these guys. They'd be friends for years, like other missionary companions, hugging at reunions and swapping photos of their kids.

"All right, slackers," he said, pretending to be cross. "How's the studying coming? Ryder?"

Plip, plip, plip went Ryder's lips, followed by a soft series of snores.

"First Corinthians, seven: one. Ryder?" Harmon persisted humorously. "Anybody?"

Gilford had not even the remotest idea, but he played along. "Hmm…" he said pensively. "It's—no, it's…. hmm." He cupped his chin and rolled his eyes toward the ceiling. "Wait…I know…it's…"

Aaron spoke up, quoting from memory: "'Having therefore these promises, dearly beloved, let us cleanse ourselves from all filthiness of the flesh and spirit, perfecting holiness in the fear of God.'"

"Wow," said Harmon. He climbed to his knees and

grabbed Aaron's face between his hands, staring sweetly, almost romantically into his eyes.

Aaron looked back with what he was certain was a recognizable—and incriminating—terror.

Harmon pulled Aaron's face close to his. "Nice going, Green. If Gilford wouldn't be completely heartbroken, you'd be my new best friend." He threw a hand over Aaron's mouth and fake-kissed him while trapping him in an inescapable wrestling headlock.

Gilford watched from his beanbag. "Hey, Harmon— I've got your heartbreak right here." Gilford grunted. His face scrunched up, his spine curled, and his colossal fart, which seemed like it must have ruptured the beanbag, brought everyone to his feet—except Ryder, that is, who had been in the middle of an equally colossal and unbelievably protracted snore. Gilford grinned across his wide face, then grimaced as his stench filled the room. "Whoo!"

Aaron tucked his Bible under one arm and laughingly ran for the front door.

Harmon rushed forward. "Holy scrud, Elder," he shouted. "You got the devil in you!" He drew back his fist and chased Gilford into the bathroom.

A second or two passed by. Ryder tossed over onto his side. His face balled up, then he bolted awake, sniffing and searching the empty room.

"Oh, man, was that me?"

Gasping for air, Aaron burst out onto the porch and sat at the top of the steps. The wind blew hard. Palm trees swayed in circles. Dry leaves, grit, and tissue paper–thin bougainvillea circlets danced along the walkways. Aaron opened his Bible, using his thumbs to hold down the pages. The wind felt good on the back of his neck. He glanced over his shoulder, over the tops of the hedges, and saw an intense orange speck in the hills. Dark smoke billowed up into a thick gray haze. News choppers hovered above, while fire-fighting helicopters with long, stem-like appendages took turns swooping down to release misty showers of flame retardant.

Suddenly Christian emerged at the top of the front steps. He crossed the courtyard with his gym bag slung across his shoulder, sucking on a smoothie from Jamba Juice. He had on those blue shorts again—and a yellow tank top. His hair stuck out in all directions, styled by the sweat of a good workout.

"Hi!" said Christian, gesturing at Aaron like they were homeboys now. "Nice game the other day."

"Thanks," said Aaron. "You guys kicked our butts."

"Ah, come on, it wasn't that bad."

"Spare me the charity." Aaron smiled. "Did you see the fire?"

"What?" Christian looked toward the hills. "Ah, man, not another one. You'll get used to it this time of year. It's the Santa Ana winds—they're deadly." Juggling his gym bag and proto-banana smoothie, Christian opened his mailbox and grabbed an armful of bills, magazines, and catalogs, which proved to be too much for him as they spilled down his abs. Squatting quickly, he captured everything at his knees, but one go-go club flyer squirted free. A strong gust immediately whirled it out to the edge of the porch. Hugging the rest of his mail at his crotch, he jerked around in his attempts to stomp on it.

Aaron grinned as the flyer sailed into the shrubbery.

"Oh, so you think that's funny, huh?" Christian dropped his gym bag, set down his smoothie, and vaulted over the handrail right into the bushes. He'd caught a glimpse of the go-go boy and thought he might know him. Christian squeezed his buff body between the stucco wall and a row of oleander bushes, bent over, and came up triumphant. He *did* know the go-go boy. Knew him well, in fact—from a very steamy encounter in the men's dressing room at the Gap. On the way back, he forgot to squeeze and just plowed forward, heedless of the scratching branches and putting on a little macho show.

"Ow! Shit! Jesus Christ!" Christian limped into the open with his hand pressed to his hip. He glanced at Aaron and caught what he perceived as his disapproval over his swearing. "Sorry, man. I must've snagged myself on the hose holder. Ow!"

"Looks like you're bleeding."

Christian removed his hand from his injury, and brought it up in front of his eyes. His fingers were smeared with blood. The color drained from his face as he quickly sat down.

"You OK?"

"Yeah, I'm fine, it's just... Just go back to your...reading."

Aaron put his nose back in his Bible, but within seconds he was startled by a series of heavy thumps. He looked up to see Christian sprawled facedown at the bottom of his front steps.

"Hey!" Aaron rushed across the courtyard and crouched over him. Was he dead or just faking? With a bit of effort, he managed to flip his gorgeous body over. Christian was out cold—but breathing. His features were slack and serene.

Aaron cradled Christian's head on his knees to improve his breathing. He tapped his cheek a few times, no response. Without thinking, he softly caressed his jaw. *So this is what he feels like.* Christian's beautiful brown eyes fluttered open, unfocused, searching—then the world filtered in.

"What?" he said, raising up on his elbow.

Aaron peered at him. "I think you, uh, fainted."

Christian furrowed his eyebrows, then sat up groggily. He looked embarrassed. "Oh—sorry, I just…I don't bleed well. I'm OK, really."

Aaron helped him to his feet. "Maybe we should get you inside," he said.

"Thanks," said Christian. "But I think I've got it from here."

"You sure?"

"Yeah, I'll be fine." He turned, swooned, and leaned heavily against the door.

Aaron threw an arm around his waist. His workout shirt was still damp from the gym, and the smell of his sweat was intoxicating. Christian's back muscles shifted under Aaron's forearm. Their hips brushed.

Aaron felt breathless. "Got the keys?" he said.

"They're in my gym bag."

"OK, hold on." He propped Christian up against the

house. "Just lean your back against the door here." He whipped around and grabbed the gym bag, holding it up. "Uh, where…?"

"In the side pocket."

Aaron set the bag down and unzipped a pocket. Staring him in the face was a handful of foil condom-wrappers—metallic blue, red, and green. Some were empty—like gum wrappers in the bottom of a woman's purse. And some were not. The keys were buried beneath them. Aaron swallowed and reached in.

"OK, here they are. Which one is it?"

"Just hand them to me, I'll show you."

Aaron handed him the keys. He gathered up the mail and jammed it under a Halloween pumpkin.

"It's this one."

Aaron took the key, then helped Christian away from the door. He tucked his head under Christian's right arm, helping him to throw it across his shoulder, then slipped his hand back around his waist and opened the door with his other hand. Suddenly Christian's legs went out from under him, and he blacked out again. Aaron held him up. In a few seconds he came to.

"Whoa, sorry."

The two staggered back, then forward.

"Wait." Aaron hesitated at the threshold. His mind raced.

I'm going in the house with him, alone. This is wrong. I shouldn't….

"Harmon!" he shouted. "Ryder! Hey, wanna give me hand out here?"

No response. Aaron hesitated again. In the hills the fire was blazing with renewed energy. A jaybird screeched his mating call from atop a nearby telephone pole. "Ka-fwee-ka-fwee-ka-fwee-ka-wee!"

A Moment of Truth

Aaron helped Christian inside.

"Which way's the bathroom?"

"Over there," panted Christian, his arm draped over Aaron's shoulder. "Down the hall and to the left."

"OK, oh, yeah—it's the same layout as ours."

"How's my ass?"

Aaron swiveled his head around to check. The stain was spreading. "Let's just get going. Don't worry, it looks fine."

When they reached the bathroom, Christian shook himself free and stumbled to the mirror, where he latched on to the chipped yellow sink and locked his elbows. The room spun around him like an amusement park ride. Deliberately, he forced himself to regard his own reflection. His face looked drained. His eyes were shiny with fear. He swallowed hard. *I have to calm myself,* he thought. He tried some deep breathing exercises. *Inhale through the nose, look up to the ceiling. Exhale through the mouth, close your eyes.*

Aaron watched him. The intimacy of witnessing such irrational fear was like nothing he'd ever felt before, like being privy to a secret ritual—only somehow more sacred, more sublime.

Christian regained his equilibrium. "Do me a favor, will ya?" he said.

"Huh?"

"I said, can you do me a favor?"

"What?"

"Take a look at it," he said through gritted teeth. "Just take a look, and tell me…you know, if I need"—he gulped loudly—"stitches."

Aaron squatted down. The stain was about the size of a silver dollar, but it didn't look like it was getting any bigger. It probably wasn't too bad, had only seemed bad because Christian had fainted. Still, he didn't want to say whether Christian needed stitches or not. How could he tell? He couldn't even see. Anyway, the situation itself was much too disconcerting for him to make a decision. He cocked his head from side to side. He lifted and lowered his hands. Could touching Christian be misconstrued?

His ass is so beautiful.

No, I did not just think that.

Aaron delicately picked at the blue spandex material. "I can't really tell."

Christian sighed. Then, in a single frantic whoosh, he slid his shorts down to his ankles—popping back up and clutching the sink stiff-armed as he kicked them off the rest of the way.

Aaron sucked in his breath at the smell of Christian's sweaty black jock, the sight of his hard, round ass. But despite the moment's obvious allure, he put on such a show of disinterest—shielding his eyes with his forearm and backing up to the wall—that he incriminated himself even further.

"What are you doing? C'mon, take a look," said Christian. "Jesus, I'm not gonna lunge at you—just take a look at it."

Embarrassed, Aaron ventured away from the wall and knelt down. "Uh, let's see here."

Christian's ass was totally bare. Only a thin black strap ran under each cheek, and a thicker black band across his hips. Aaron made an effort to concentrate on the wound, which was about an inch and a half long, but not very deep. Most of the blood had already come off on Christian's shorts, which now lay in a tiny powder-blue wad at the base of the toilet.

"Well?" said Christian.

"Uh, let's see here… Do you have a washcloth?"

"There's one in the cabinet. Hey, how's it look?"

"Not sure yet," said Aaron. "Which cabinet?"

"On the wall," said Christian, "behind me."

Aaron stood. He opened the cabinet and was immediately charmed. He stared in fascination at an array of neatly—almost artistically—arranged hair and grooming products along with three rows of perfectly stacked yellow, green, and white washcloths. Aaron selected a white one and closed the cabinet. He turned and bent to twist the hot water faucet handle, testing the tepid stream that came out.

Christian watched Aaron's strong hands as they soaked the steaming washcloth and wrung it out over the sink. He glanced at Aaron's face. He was beautiful when he was nervous.

Aaron got on his knees again. He swiped at the pale,

olive skin around the cut, clearing away some dried blood.

Christian tensed and hissed sharply.

"That hurts?"

"No, I'm just anticipating."

Aaron dabbed the cut gently.

"Is it bad?" asked Christian, his voice nearly a wail.

"I don't think so. No, it's fine...just a little scratch."

Christian turned to have a look. Oops, no thanks. He leaned hard on the sink, swallowing a rush of bile. "Whew," he said, gagging. "That's great news."

Aaron looked up at him. "Got any disinfectant?"

Christian gripped the sink with his left hand, pulled open the medicine cabinet with his right, and passed Aaron a bottle of peroxide.

"This is gonna sting a little." Aaron wondered if Christian would pass out again. Then he wondered if he himself might pass out. The stress was too much for him, and he began to ramble as he cleaned out the cut. "Funny, I'm not squeamish. In high school we went to this hospital. I was the only kid who wanted to watch surgery. So they helped me scrub down, and then they gave me a set of scrubs—you know, those green things?—to put on and everything...got a Band-Aid?"

Christian handed down a small box.

Aaron opened it and pulled one out.

"So anyway," he went on, peeling away the paper, "I got to watch as they opened this guy's chest. And there it was. This heart, you know? This human heart."

He fidgeted around in the box for a second Band-Aid.

"You think about it beating and all, but it's more of a

dance. And I couldn't get over that that's all that tethers us to this planet—this one fragile muscle. And how it's so tiny, really, in the big scheme of things. And when you think about all the things that can stop it…well, you just figure that there's got to be something else, something miraculous that keeps that valiant little muscle dancing." He glanced up at Christian, whose face had turned a disturbing pistachio-green. "You know?"

A thin film of sweat had formed on Christian's upper lip. His breathing came rapid and shallow. His eyes were clamped shut as he tried but was unable to shake from his mind's eye the image of a fragile blood-soaked heart.

Aaron blushed. "Sorry," he said. "I'll stop talking now."

Christian opened his eyes and nodded. Wet locks of hair clung to his forehead. His pupils seemed to drift then center again. "I think I need to lie down."

Aaron helped Christian into his bedroom. The walls were cherry-red and decorated with a number of assorted empty picture frames. The only piece of actual artwork was over the bed—a giant yellow canvas with an abstract sketch in black acrylic paint of a man's genitals. The bed was draped with a white sheepskin throw. A shelf over the bed contained a variety of baubles—a bowling pin, a fishbowl with some condoms in it, a hunk of pink coral, a plastic hula dancer, a Chick Hearn bobblehead, and a lavender Tinkie Winkie being fellated by Barbie.

Christian reached forward and climbed onto his bed, sprawling out on the sheepskin like a shipwrecked castaway—facedown, ass up. "Ugh," he groaned. "It's hot, hot…I'm hot." He rolled to one side, sat up, and peeled off his shirt. Glistening with a sweaty sheen, his muscular torso served as the perfect backdrop to the stirring black bulge in his jock. As he lay back, his abs puffed out like a row of muffins in the oven. The boy was stacked.

Aaron tried to keep his wits about him. "Maybe I'll get you a c-cool cloth," he mumbled.

"Yeah," Christian moaned dramatically. "That sounds good."

Aaron bolted into the bathroom. It was safe there. Grabbing a fresh washcloth from the cabinet, he set it on the edge of the sink. He then ran cold water into his hands and splashed his face. Three large drops of water fell onto his gray T-shirt, leaving dark splotches as he stared at himself in the mirror.

He knew he should leave.

He did not want to leave.

Christian lay flat on his back, his chest rising and falling peacefully as he listened to Aaron splash around in his bathroom. He closed his eyes, took some deep calming breaths, and let the rest of the tension run out of him.

Aaron entered the room with his arms held tightly against his body and the cold cloth poised like a fig leaf over his loins.

Christian lounged sensually before him—eyes closed, one knee drawn up, his arm stretched out across the cloud-like throw as if reaching to touch God's hand.

Aaron sat on the bed.

Christian felt part of the mattress sink down and kept his eyes shut.

Aaron held the cool white washcloth in his lap. He

studied Christian's face: wide nose, dark eyelashes, eyelids that were lovely as a sunset, prominent cheekbones, lips resting in a half-smile. And wait a minute…were his eyebrows waxed? Aaron was certain that they were, and for some reason he felt endeared to the notion. He watched the hypnotic rise and fall of Christian's chest and the faint, vulnerable thumping of his heart.

Aaron dabbed Christian's cheeks and forehead. Somehow he managed to convince himself that he was here because he needed to be, and that his ministrations were purely platonic. He pulled Christian's arm into his lap and pressed the cloth against his wrist.

Christian opened his eyes.

Aaron brought the cloth back up to his forehead. "You're hot," he said.

Christian reached up to cover Aaron's hand with his own, dragging the cloth down over his nose, his lips…

Aaron breathed deeply. What was he doing? Where were they going with this?

Christian pulled Aaron's hand along, dragging the washcloth over his chin. He tilted his head, as if guzzling some drink, and guided it down the fragile terrain of his throat. As the cloth grazed his chiseled chest, the two of them inhaled sharply. He brought his other hand up to help guide Aaron's trapped hand down over his steaming abs, down over his…

Aaron shook with desire.

Christian took one hand away from the cloth and slipped it behind Aaron's neck. His fingers grazed the soft, short hair at the base of Aaron's skull. Slowly, he guided Aaron's face to his.

Each tasted the other's warm breath.

Eyes wide, Aaron pulled back suddenly, then just as suddenly collapsed on top of Christian, burying his face in that muscular chest, hiding like a scared child. "I haven't...I haven't done anything...anything like this. I haven't..."

Christian cradled Aaron's head. It felt so sweet there against his chest. He lowered his voice. "It's OK," he soothed. "This doesn't have to mean anything."

Aaron lifted his head. "Yes, it does."

"Shh... It could be just a little fun between friends."

"My first time could be just a little fun for you?" Aaron pulled back.

Christian raised himself up onto his elbows. "No, don't get all..." But he was too late.

"All what?" Aaron shouted. "Maybe you can equate sex with a handshake and that's what? Like a badge? What— do you want me to congratulate you?"

Christian felt defensive. "Hey, don't you preach to me, OK? Who are you, some kid from the sticks? You come in here and you think you can fucking judge me?"

"Oh, yeah," said Aaron, pushing himself off the bed. "I'm just some doodah pudknocker from Pocatello. They ship us here from Dork Island."

Newly endeared, Christian scrunched up his face. "What?"

"I'm saying I know how retarded you think I am, OK?" Aaron faced the wall and dropped his forehead against it. "You've found me out, all right? My worst secret. I'm humiliated now, so...your work is done here." He began to cry.

"Wait," said Christian. "I don't think you're a dork."

Aaron sniffled loudly.

"It's just that…well, your religion makes you act like one."

Aaron turned. His features twisted as he struggled with his anger. "Don't you believe in anything?"

"Yeah. Of course I do."

"Then tell me! You tell me one thing in your life, one thing beyond a shadow of a doubt that you really and truly believe."

"I believe…" Christian gazed at the ceiling a moment. "I firmly believe that Ann Margret has never been given her due as an actress."

"Duh," said Aaron, "for *Tommy* alone—and did you see when she played…?" He paused, catching himself. "BUT IS THAT SOMETHING YOU CAN BUILD A LIFE ON?!"

Christian thought this over. It seemed remotely feasible.

"Look at yourself," said Aaron. "You're so pretty and colorful on the outside, but inside you're nothing but fluff. You're like a walking, talking marshmallow Peep!"

"Hey…that's not fair."

"When it's true, it doesn't matter." Aaron paused, looking around at the empty frames on the walls. "I can't believe what I was about to do, when there is nothing, Christian, *nothing* about you that's not skin-deep."

Christian listened to Aaron's footsteps across the floor. As the door shut, he became sharply aware of himself. What if Aaron had been right? What if he was nothing more than a naked piece of fluff?

Aaron stood, bewildered, on the porch of Christian's bungalow. The unzipped gym bag next to his foot, the smoothie cup at the bottom of the steps, and the pile of mail under the pumpkin were all still there to remind him that what could never have happened just did. It was still windy, though balmier now than before. In the hills, the fire had been successfully extinguished, and the sky was a smoky pink. Windblown eucalyptus bark and the smolder from the brushfire combined for a smell that reminded him of the cedar chips his mother used in his sweater drawer at home.

Aaron trotted down the steps to cross the courtyard and retrieve his Bible. The heavy black book waited in the same spot he'd left it. He picked it up, opened it to a random page, and stared—hurting with the guilt of having abandoned a constant companion. He read: *How happy is the one who does not follow the advice of the wicked, or stand in the pathway with sinners...*

He straightened up, then paused at the door of his bungalow. "OK," he told himself softly, resignedly. "Nothing happened." He closed his book and carried it inside.

Ryder was still snoring on the couch. Down the hall, in the bathroom, Gilford had backed Harmon up against the sink.

"Dang it, Elder," said Gilford. "I'm gonna hit ya, and it's gonna hurt."

"I don't even know what pain is," Harmon told him.

Gilford popped him in the arm, a solid right.

Harmon grabbed his shoulder and doubled over. "Ow! Ow, gol-dangit, that hurt!"

"I warned you," Gilford smirked, walking off down the hall.

Aaron stood surveying the scene. How could nothing have changed? He went into the bathroom and locked the door.

Starbuck's on Sunset was full of young hipsters in shades and lowslung jeans. A Nina Simone song from their jazz compilation was playing.

Julie sipped her latte. "Long or thick?" she asked.

"Thick," answered Traci.

"Crooked or straight?"

"Straight…mm, well…yeah, straight, definitely."

"Hairy or not so hairy?"

"Not so."

"What about pierced?"

"Not pierced," said Traci. "I've never even seen pierced. Have you?"

Julie smirked. "Maybe."

"Maybe?"

"Well…remember John?"

"John had a pierced cock?"

"Shh…could you keep it down?"

"John had a pierced cock?" Traci whispered. "But he was so normal."

"The man was a born-again Christian—and he still had a Prince Albert, OK?"

"Ugh," said Traci. "I don't get it. Aren't men getting distracted by their dicks, like, nonstop already? Do they really need to be reminded?"

"Oh, stop," said Julie, holding her stomach. "You're hurting me. Hey, whatever happened to that part you were up for?"

"Didn't get it," said Traci. "And I don't want to talk about it."

"That's fine," said Julie.

"All I know," said Traci, "is that I need to find a niche."

"OK."

"You know, like you have a niche."

"You mean the black niche?"

"That's exactly what I mean. You have the black niche. Christian has the gay niche. And I have the jack-shit niche."

"So you're telling me that being black is an advantage?"

"No, I'm telling you it's a niche. Just like blond is a niche, sporty brunette is a niche, bitchy Asian is a niche."

"OK, how about New York Jew—isn't that a niche?"

Traci looked at her. "Duh, if you're short—but I'm 5-foot-11."

"Well, isn't Lisa Kudrow Jewish?"

"I'm not sure. But if she is, she's in the insanely long-necked niche, not the Jewish-girl niche. The jewish-girl niche is strictly for shorties. Tall Jewish women are way too scary for Hollywood."

"So you need a niche, huh?"

"That's what I'm saying, and if I don't get one soon, I'm going to have to do something drastic."

The bathroom mirror wore a coat of steam. Drops streaked down the center like tears. Behind the shower door, hot water pounded Aaron's chest as he braced himself with his left hand and his right arm swayed rhythmically near his hip. He was thinking of Christian, of the pure white cloth that touched his wound, of his beautiful ass, that ridiculous jock, of how it had felt to throw his arms around another man and confess...and confess.... Aaron hung his head. The shower beat down on the back of his neck. *I've never done anything like this... It doesn't have to mean anything...* Suddenly, savagely, he threw his head back, exposing his chest and throat. Grabbing the faucet handle, he jolted the water to cold, gasped, and dropped to his knees, bruising them on the tile. "No," he whispered. "No." And then he prayed.

A Question of Faith

Another night was winding down at Lila's. Carlos, the chef, had stepped outside for a cigarette. Julie sat in a curved booth for six, stuffing sprigs of silk daffodils into vases, as Traci stood over a nearby table separating a pile of silverware and Andrew counted out tips at the bar. Christian placed a bread plate on a table, put his hands on his hips, and studied it. "Do you believe in God?" he asked.

"What?" Julie twisted her head in several different directions, as if tracking a fly. "Who are you talking to?"

"You," said Christian, walking over and scooting in next to her. "No, everybody. All right, this is a general question: Do any of you believe in God?"

Andrew stepped out from behind the bar. "You mean," he said, smiling, "other than Madonna?"

The clatter of dishes being sprayed down in the kitchen echoed across the restaurant. Something—a pot lid, probably—fell to the floor, rolled out from under the swinging doors, and spun in one place.

"Fuckin'-A," said Traci. "Yeah, I believe in God. Why not?"

Julie wove a daffodil into her braids. "I don't know," she said, her eyes suddenly spacey and her features slack. It was as if the mere question had thrown her back in time, back to her Malibu flower-childhood, when the enlightened Guru Yangru used to stay at the house and would take her mother through mind-releasing meditations. "I believe"—she sighed—"in harmony, as a law of the universe, like gravity."

Traci nodded, lulled into agreement.

"You know," Julie continued, placing her palms together. "It's like we're meant to vibrate together."

Andrew came over and sat at the top corner of the booth. He crossed his arms over his lap and looked contemplative. "Hey, being positive since I was 17 sort of gives meaning to the word "miracle"—so yeah, without getting all holy on your ass, I believe. Why?"

Julie aimed a thumb at Christian and rolled her eyes. "The Mormons are mind-fucking him."

"Ha!" shouted Traci, scooting in next to Christian. "I should've guessed."

"Oh, honey," laughed Andrew, swinging his legs over and facing the group. He pointed a finger at Christian. "You do not want to let them get into your psyche. You might start off just listening to Amy Grant, but then before you know it, it's 3 A.M. and you've got your VISA card and you're giving it to that scary bitch on TV with the big lavender hair."

"Mm-huh," added Julie. "You better testify. I mean, hello, Christian, we've got a bet going on here." She nudged him with her elbow. "It's you convert one of them, not the other way around, remember?"

"Whoa, whoa, whoa!" Christian put up his hands. "Did you forget who you're talking to? You want to change your bet, missy? Go right ahead. I'll bus all your damn tables then, *if* I lose this—but let me just say…"

"No, no," said Andrew, "let *me* just say…I dated this guy once who was an actor. Cute Southern boy. Came from this real religious family…"

"Hello, I'm seeing a pattern here," said Traci.

"If you mean, do I dig uptight choirboys? Answer's yes."

Julie laughed. "Just don't tell me he jumped all over your azaleas."

"No, thank God—but when his parents found out he was gay…" Andrew threw up his hands. "Can you say 'drama'?"

Traci raised an eyebrow. "Oh, no—did they put his wee-wee in the shock box?"

"Honey," said Andrew, "it was much worse than that. They ended up sending him to one of those Christian 'change' ministries where they try to beef up your masculinity by making you learn to fix cars and watch Monday-night football. Forked over a lot of dough for it too."

"Wow," said Traci. "So, did he change?"

"Did he?" Andrew snapped his fingers. "Miss Thang used to be a top!"

"Shut up!"

"I'm not kidding—he's still gayer than a box of birds."

"Box of birds," said Traci. "I love that."

"How about he's twirlier than a party dress? But seriously, it fucked with him. This religion shit always does."

"Look," said Christian. "I'm not being fucked with. It's just…" He paused, trying hard to produce some sort of meaningful expression. "I'm not…shallow—am I?"

A prolonged silence followed. Julie pretended to check the integrity of her fingernail polish.

"Honey, you don't have to be deep," Traci told him. She patted his arm. "You just have to be pretty."

Christian looked devastated.

"OK, Traci," said Julie. "I don't think you're helping."

"Look," said Andrew. "If you have something to prove—fine. Be at my house tomorrow at 6:30 in the morning."

"Six-thirty in the morning?" Christian laughed nervously. "You gotta be kidding. Why?"

"Why?" said Andrew. "Because you're gonna have to sacrifice if you want to find yourself—or get over yourself, or whatever it is you're doing." He swung his long legs over the top of the seat, jumped down from the booth, and headed back toward the bar.

Christian watched him. "You don't think I'll be there, do you?"

"Your words," said Andrew, shrugging. "Not mine."

Christian could not quite get it.

At 6:07 A.M., in front of his bathroom mirror, he was practicing looking unshallow. He had been there since 5:30, having been unable to sleep over the idea that there was actually something wrong with him—an identified flaw!—and, to his credit, he had worked very hard and produced some very interesting expressions, many of them involving facial muscles he'd never even known about. Unfortunately, none had made him look like anything even remotely "deep."

The trick was to erase all vanity, then replace it with sincerity—which was the part that kept tripping him up. He tried again. No—too Mother Teresa. Again—nope. One more try…a little more narrowing of the eyes…yes.

"By Jove," he whispered to his new self. "I think you've got it."

And so, on a very gray Tuesday morning, in a pair of wrinkled jeans, hair flat and unwashed, an old striped polo shirt that fit him funny, and last year's shades, a very gray though still not-so-deep-looking Christian dragged himself down the steps of the courtyard to find Aaron and his missionary companion, Ryder, on the sidewalk strapping on their bike helmets.

Christian caught Aaron's eye.

"Hey," he said, trying out his new expression.

"Hey," said Aaron, and quickly looked away.

Fuck him, fumed Christian. *I'm not shallow.*

Aaron tried to keep his eyes off Christian. Whenever his eyes did meet his neighbor's gorgeous brown ones, or brush across his chest, or linger on his legs, or on his perfect round ass, he felt pummeled by an avalanche of emotion. He couldn't help it, but he'd been praying on it.

God hadn't spared him yet.

He wondered why Christian had looked at him like that—like he'd just gotten hit with a bad case of the runs. Aaron hoped he wasn't the cause. But then, he was not supposed to feel concerned or protective—and forget about aroused. Did Christian show up specifically to torture him? Well, if he *did*, it worked. Aaron had never felt so self-conscious in his life. His armpits were damp, his trousers were one size too small on one side, and as he threw his leg over the seat of his bicycle, he sensed acutely that his ankles were showing above his socks. Pedaling off, he remembered the homeless man he'd seen at the side of the freeway near the airport on his first night in the city. Maybe his sign had been right—and Los Angeles really was hell.

Clutching his Starbucks stainless-steel travel carafe, Christian readjusted his shoulder bag. He watched, blurry-eyed, as Aaron and Ryder mounted their cycles and pedaled off down the block. He took a sip of coffee and shook his head. If they were out of the house at this hour every morning, no wonder that Ryder guy was such a big sourpuss.

It was all about Aaron, of course. Christian had never experienced such an indefinable madness.

He was falling in love.

With a pen behind his ear and a clipboard under his arm, Andrew proudly strolled along the rear loading deck of Project Angel Food's central kitchen. "Christian, I bet you didn't know this, but all of our meals are prepared by professional chefs…"

"Oh, really?" said Christian, without really hearing. Ten minutes into his tour of the facility, he was busy trying to remember how he knew the hot, thick-necked bald guy handing up crates of vegetables from the back of a white delivery van. *George?* he wondered silently. *Is that you, Jumbo Jock?*

"Hey, there, beauty queen," said Andrew. "Pay

attention to the task at hand, OK? I don't have all day to go over this stuff."

Christian rubbed the crud from his eyes. "Hey, I got up at 5:30 to be here on time—cut me some slack, will you?"

"Look, quit bitching." Andrew surveyed his clipboard. "It's the early bird that catches the worm."

"Oh, now, there's an incentive. Who cares about a worm when you can get pizza till 3?"

Andrew aimed his pen at him. "OK, here's the deal. I'm gonna take you around to see a few more things. Once we finish up your training, there'll be a half-hour of cutting and chopping, then we'll set you up with a route."

"A route?" whined Christian. "On my first day?"

"Come on," said Andrew. "You're delivering food. It's what you do already—only this time you're driving." He clapped Christian on the back. "Think of yourself as a waiter on wheels."

"Great." Christian sighed. "If I were in hot pants and roller skates, this would be the fulfillment of a dream."

Andrew looked him up and down. "For all of us."

Door-to-Door

Aaron and Ryder approached the front door of a well-kept craftsman home in Echo Park. There was something so friendly about its tidy porch. Flower boxes and humming-bird feeders hung from the eaves. The mailbox was shaped like a teddy bear's head. Ryder opened the screen door. Aaron knocked. They felt good about this one.

A middle-aged man in a red velour bathrobe answered. He looked from one missionary to the other.

"Good morning," said Aaron. "We're here from the Church of Jesus Christ of…"

The man held up his finger. "Just a moment. Honey!" he shouted off to the side. "Stacy, could you come out here, please. You'll want to hear this."

They listened to the sound of a shower being turned off.

Aaron tossed Ryder a "this is working out" look. They shared a moment of godly serenity—a mutual hunch that filled them with grace. Their day was going great so far. The 7 A.M. discussion with the Ramos family had gone off like a charm. Mrs. Ramos had served them a plateful of delicious little cakes. And now this.

Heavy footsteps thudded across the floor.

The man smiled apologetically. Finally Stacy arrived from the shower.

Aaron opened his mouth. His jaw moved, but no sound came out.

Ryder put his hand on his stomach and swallowed.

A 6-foot-6, hard-bodied man in a skimpy, threadbare towel stood in front of them. His wet hair sent drops down his neck and chest. His skin was red with a post-shower sheen. "Well, well, well," he said. "What have we here?!"

"Uh…" said Ryder, turning away. "Never mind."

Stacy flashed Aaron a knowing smile. His boyfriend whipped his head around, caught it, and jealously smacked him on the chest.

As the flustered missionaries descended the walkway, the robed man called after them. "Sure you boys don't want to come in for some coffee? A nice mimosa, maybe?"

"Project Angel Food. Hello?" Christian stood with his ear to the door of a two-story Silver Lake Victorian. The large grocery bag he held under one arm was folded over and stapled shut at the top with a square of paper that read #47. Dangling near his head on three wires was a half-browned plant in a ceramic pot. He knocked again, then spied a ringer near the door. He twisted it. *Brrring!*

"Hello! Project Angel…"

"I said, come in," rasped a voice.

Christian opened the door and entered the house. It was dark inside. And it smelled bad. But Christian had been inside more than one dark, foul-smelling living space that day. What surprised him was the size and underlying elegance beneath the clutter. Still, the Tiffany lamp and other high-end furnishings were covered in a thick layer of dust. And the baby grand in the corner was littered with a 3-foot stack of books, old newspapers, and magazines, on top of which lay open Tupperware containers with fork handles sticking out and small swarms of fruit flies circling above.

"Hello? Keith?"

"I said 'come in' three goddamned times."

Christian turned and saw in the farthest corner the dark silhouette of a man in a black hooded sweatshirt. He was seated in a low-slung, oversize easy chair with his socked feet on an ottoman and a blanket covering his lap. Nearby was a small window with its curtains pulled. The steady puff of an oxygen tank ticked like slow seconds through the room.

"Sorry," said Christian. "I didn't hear you." He held up the bag, looking around for an inch of free space. "Where do you want me to put this?"

"I don't care," Keith said, without looking up. "I'm not hungry."

"OK, well, uh…" Christian took off his sunglasses. "Maybe if I could just turn a light on…" The lamp chain felt cold in his hand. He pulled it down—*click*—then released it. A third of the room swam in yellowish light. Keith glanced up, his gaunt face fully visible. His sunken hazel eyes, their lower lids gaping and wound-red, drifted up to Christian's and filled with an unpleasant recognition. Attached to the grimy oxygen tank sitting next to him, an aqua-tinted plastic tube made a loop-de-loop on its way to his chapped nostrils, invading them with its truncated prongs. *Puff-sssss, puff-ssss.* The sound of the oxygen entering the man's nose, combined with the sight of a dime-size purplish splotch on his forehead, filled Christian with the sudden overwhelming urge to throw his arms up and run.

But instead he stared straight into his client's eyes.

Keith lowered his voice. His dark hair grew in fuzzy patches on his head. "You're not gonna last long if you look that shocked with everybody."

Christian's gaze dropped to the floor. He just wanted to get this over with, and he wandered into the center of the room. "I'll just put this down"—he paused to move a pile of newspapers and a half-eaten apple off the top of a TV tray—"here." The crackle of the bag seemed painfully magnified.

"So," said Keith, "got a cigarette?"

Christian cleared his throat and laughed uncomfortably. "Um, isn't that an oxygen tank?"

Keith glanced at the tank. He nodded.

"So, couldn't it…uh…explode?"

Keith gave a scratchy cackle and mimicked a small explosion with his fingers. "*Boom.* That'd be such a terrible way to go, wouldn't it? So, come on," he said, letting his hands fall to his lap. "How 'bout that cigarette?"

"Sorry," said Christian, side-stepping toward the door. "I don't smoke."

"Wait," Keith wheezed. "Can I ask you a question?"

Christian stopped. "I guess."

"What are you doing here?"

"I'm delivering your food—I thought you'd been through the routine."

"No, no, no—I mean *you.* You pretty boys usually

don't do shit like this. So what is it? Are you punishing yourself for something?" Keith narrowed his bloodshot eyes. "Feel guilty for being so good-looking when there are so many ugly fucks in the world, that it?"

"I, uh...I don't..."

"Did you get tired of doing reps at the gym?" Keith went on. "And bragging about your latest conquests and all the rest of your stupid shallow little life?"

A dark look came across Christian's face. "Fuck you. You don't know me." He turned and headed for the door.

"Of course I do." Keith's jagged laugh bounced off the walls of the apartment and died amid the clutter. "I used to *be* you."

Christian halted. He faced Keith with tightened lips.

"Yeah," said Keith. "That's right. I had a career, friends, looks, the whole package." He sighed dramatically. "But now I'm just a skeletal reminder that we might only be in the eye of the hurricane." Keith stared ominously at Christian and began to make a sound: "Ehhhhhhhhh."

"Yeah, whatever, bud," said Christian. "I'm outta here."

"Ehhhhhhhhhh....ha, ha, ha...I'm just fucking with you, man." Keith chuckled happily, holding up his hand. "I'm sorry, man, ha, ha, you should've seen your face. No, wait. Sorry, I get bored sitting around here, so I like to rattle the newbies. I must look like shit, because it didn't ever used to be this easy." He shifted in his chair. "Could you just please help me get this pillow under me? I don't know, I can't...I can't..."

Christian took his hands off his hips and walked over to him.

"Swear to Christ, my butt's wasted away to nothing. Too bad"—he winked—"I used to have a killer ass. I've got pictures of it somewhere around here somewhere." Keith reached ahead for a dust-smothered photo album on the coffee table. He couldn't quite get to it and lost his balance, falling forward. Christian grabbed his elbow to steady him, and slid the cushion into place.

"Killer ass," he said. "I'll take your word for it." As he helped Keith settle back into the chair, Keith latched on to his tricep for support. They froze like this for a moment, immobilized by a painful surge of current that passed between them.

"Snow," said Keith, his eyes rolled back, his grip tightening. "It's all just...snow."

Christian wrenched his arm away. "What did you just say?"

"I'm sorry," said Keith. "Maybe it's the meds, but...sometimes I just get this weird read on people." He paused to catch his breath, cradled his forehead on his fingertips, and swiveled his eyes up to meet Christian's. "But you're like a blank TV screen. All I see is snow. What do you suppose that means?"

"Nothing." Christian backed his way to the door. "Nothing...I'll see you around."

"No, you won't," said Keith. "Enjoy your pretty life..."

Christian opened the door and stepped out.

"...while it's still pretty."

The door closed behind him, latching like the lid of a coffin. Christian leaned back against it and stared at the sunlit bark of a pine tree in the front yard. It was a beautiful pink persimmon-colored light. He went to remove his sunglasses but was surprised to find they weren't on. Christian stepped off the porch and looked up. The sky was full of smoke. The sun glared through it like an angry red eye.

Keith sat alone in the dark for a few minutes before reaching under an end table for a small pouch of fine white powder.

Due to the combined hazards of bark beetles, four years of draught, raging Santa Ana winds, the suppression of natural fires, and an arsonist or two, the first of four major Southern California brushfires was raging that morning in San Bernadino County. The haze above Los Angeles was thick as soup.

Silhouettes backlit by a cantaloupe sky, two helmeted young men in white dress shirts with dark ties and slacks pedaled their secondhand 10-speeds along one of the lesser-trafficked side streets of Echo Park. Aaron's forehead was beaded with sweat. His navy slacks clung to his legs. His shoes—polished that morning—were coated with white flecks of ash.

Wheezing and huffing 20 feet back, Ryder called out, "Hey, slow down, Davis. This ain't the flippin' Tour de France."

Aaron coasted to a stop at the curb, where he waited in the shade of a giant elm, tripping on the way everything looked in the oddly beautiful light.

Ryder pulled up next to him. He waved his arms like a

coach in the face of an incompetent umpire. "Just what do you think you're doing, Greenie? We're supposed to stick together. Or do the rules not matter to you?"

"Sorry," said Aaron. "I was thinking about something and forgot where I was."

"Well, you ought to be thinking about what you're doing."

"I know…I will. Hey!" Aaron nodded to a sign beneath the elm: HOSPICE CENTER.

"Yeah," said Ryder with narrowed eyes. "So?"

"So, I think we should maybe go in."

"Oh, no," said Ryder, starting off on his bike. "No way."

But something about this cluster of crisp white cottages amid soft, mellow-green grass was calling to Aaron. And, as a priest of God, he was duty-bound to trust himself in these moments. Some of the most profound conversion stories in the church's history were guided by small moments like this—powerful urges that were the Heavenly Father's way of taking over and working through his followers. *Lord,* prayed Aaron. *Reveal to me your will, for I am but your tool.*

Ryder had already pedaled ahead 10 feet before he realized his junior companion hadn't budged. He braked to a halt, put one foot on the ground, and twisted around on his bike seat. "What the….?"

"Come on," said Aaron, grinning. "We should at least try…"

"Ah, for the love of flippin' Pete," shouted Ryder. "We're not tracting a hospice. That's full-on sick—and not in a good way."

But Aaron was already pedaling onto the path that led through the grounds. "We'll just go up to the main building—see if they'll let us put some pamphlets in the lobby."

With a frustrated sigh, Ryder climbed off his bike. He walked it back to the curb, wheeled it up over the edge, and leaned the frame against the elm. He wiped his forehead on his sleeve, looking around at the weirdly lit lawn. It was a cool, shady spot, with hard, black dirt and spiky tufts of green grass, and his thin legs were tired.

Aaron waited on the path, like a dog expecting his owner to follow.

Ryder pressed his back against the tree and crossed his arms and legs. "Oh, no," he said. "You're dancing solo on this one, cowboy."

Aaron wobbled off, his front tire twisting back and forth to keep balance at the slow pace. He was certain about the rightness of reaching out to the dying. It was clearly the compassionate and Christlike thing to do.

Ryder unhooked and pulled off his helmet, plopped his butt down onto a tree root, and rested back against the elm's trunk. It was scratchy and cool against his ribs. Let Davis go on in there and waste his time if he wanted to; he wasn't going to suffer another second of that kid's ignorance. Ryder liked Elder Davis, but he'd have liked him a lot more if he weren't always acting like such a high and mighty goober. When it came down to actually doing something—like having a tough talk with that gay guy next door—the kid was useless, a total lightweight. "He's probably a big old homo himself," muttered Ryder. A flake of ash flew into his mouth and married itself to his tongue. Ryder spit it out bitterly. Suddenly, as he closed his eyes, the face of Misty Johnson appeared—freckled and pale, with her flipped-back mousy-brown hair. *Misty Johnson,* he thought with a sigh. Now, there was a woman. Hadn't he loved her since the very first moment he saw her? She was the prettiest, smartest, most sensitive girl he had ever known...

They'd met at the Latter Day Saints Institution on campus at the University of Utah. He knew after their first date that he had fallen in love with her. As they ate their burgers at Hires in Salt Lake, he noticed how casually she ate, and how often her long hair fell into the corners of her lips, in frequent danger of being devoured. She talked a lot, but not nervously. She had confidence and said that she would be a public orator one day—that there just didn't seem to be enough public orators in America. He liked her ideas—he thought she was amusing. He had always liked smart and sassy girls.

Misty hadn't come from the best Mormon family. You could hardly even call them Mormon. They had all been baptized, but both of her parents had been partiers—drinking and smoking with the country club crowd. She told him about how they had once taken a houseboat out on Lake Powell one summer. Misty's dad had crashed it into a rock, and her mother had gone flying through the sliding-glass door. Her dad and his drunken friends had used vodka to kill the pain from the cut over her eye. Her sister had married a Jew, and her brother had renounced the church as soon as he returned from his mission. Ryder thought he might have to encourage Misty's faith a little. Her family would certainly be no help.

But none of that had ever mattered to Ryder. What mattered was how Misty had made him feel, which was like he was 10 feet tall and the funniest guy in the world.

A minute later, near the rear of the complex, a disappointed Aaron exited the main building. "Hey, Ryder! Ryder!"

Ryder opened his eyes. He spotted Aaron across the lot, small as a speck. "What?"

Aaron cupped his hand to his mouth. "They only take nondenominational literature in the lobby!"

"Well, what did I flippin' tell you?"

Aaron felt humiliated. *So much for God's will,* he thought woefully. But as he pushed his bike along, he saw an elegant woman coming his way.

Lila Montagne wore a brown felt hat and a beige linen wrap around her shoulders. Her sandals dragged along the concrete. Her arms were flush with her slender torso as she clutched the thin strap of her purse with both hands. She tightened her lips and kept her head lowered as she passed Aaron on the walkway.

Aaron stopped and turned to watch her as she pulled herself along a few more feet, then sagged like a deflated party balloon onto a nearby bench in the shade of a pair of smooth-barked palms. She sobbed audibly.

"Ma'am? Are you OK?"

Lila looked up at him, and it took Aaron a moment to recover from the shock of her beauty and charisma.

"Are you all right?"

She nodded yes, but her face crumpled, and she began to wail.

Aaron turned his bike on its side on the grass. He walked to the bench, then stood in uncertain silence at her side. She smelled of a woman's tears—like damp make-up—and of lack of sleep, and of worry. He sat next to her, about two feet away. "Is there anything I can do?"

"I…" She looked at him again. "I don't do this." And it took her a moment, but she composed herself. She sat up straight and assumed an almost aristocratic bearing. "That's better," she said. Then, placing her thin hand lightly on his knee as if to console him for his concern, she added, "I don't normally… I am not…one to cry at weddings. I just don't. And I refuse to break down in front of strangers. Even when someone—probably the most important person in my life—has just died…"

Aaron glanced anxiously in Ryder's direction, but Ryder was sacked out against the tree, his chin resting heavily on his rising and falling chest.

Lila sobbed. She lifted her face to the sky and bawled.

Aaron felt at a loss. He adjusted the strap of his shoulder bag and tried to be calm and present with the woman. He looked at her and said earnestly, "I'm so sorry."

Lila glanced at him. "Oh, he would have hated to see me cry like this," she said. "Henry hated public outbursts. He and Bogdanovich used to tell me, 'Save it for the camera.'"

Aaron forgot himself. "You know Peter Bogdanovich?"

"Oh, you're sweet"—she sniffled—"letting me drop names. Kids like you don't even know who he is."

Aaron shook his head and smiled. "I've seen *The Last Picture Show* only 37 times."

Lila tried to be interested, but then buried her face in her hands. "It's all wrong," she moaned. "Young man, this should have happened in the dark of night. I shouldn't have had to do this. He shouldn't have made me do this…" She reached for his hand and clung to it. "Just"— she swallowed a sob—"turning it all off and letting him go like that."

Aaron watched her. She stared ahead, lost in recent memory.

"Just…waiting there, watching that line on the little screen go straight." She laughed ironically. "He always said television would be the death of him."

"Who was he?" asked Aaron. "Your husband?"

"No—well, never my official husband. Then again…probably my best friend. Certainly my best director." She swiped delicately under one eye with her little finger. "The parts he encouraged me to take were always the most difficult, always the least obvious choices." Lila paused, with a wry sideways look, at which point Aaron suddenly recognized her.

Lila Montagne!

But he did nothing—or at least he hoped he did nothing—to indicate this.

"His doctor called to let me know when it was time, and that they'd moved him here, that this was what he wanted." She broke down a second time. "I should've been prepared."

Aaron moved closer. From his pocket, he offered her a fresh linen handkerchief.

She took it, peering at him with appreciative curiosity.

"I haven't had a gentleman offer me a real handkerchief in years. Who are you, Cary Grant?"

Aaron blushed. "No, ma'am. I'm a Mormon missionary."

Lila's tears mixed with laughter. "Then I'd say we've gone from the tragic to the sublime. Good heavens, look at the sky—there must be some kind of brushfire somewhere."

"It's in San Bernadino," said Aaron. "We saw it on the news at this house we were visiting. An arsonist set it. It's amazing, isn't it, what one guy with a match can do?"

"An arsonist. Well, that's just terrible." Lila tried to put on a brave face. "So, you're a Mormon missionary. If only I'd run into you a few minutes earlier, I suppose you could have done the last rites."

"Oh," said Aaron, laughing. "We don't do that. We just pass out pamphlets…and they give us these discussions that we memorize. That's why I'm not really sure what to say here." He paused, then tentatively took her hand. "Do you ever read the Sunday comics?"

Lila looked at him. "I beg your pardon?"

Aaron smiled. "The comics page?"

Slowly, beautifully, Lila's expression turned into that of a small girl being told a bedtime story after a nightmare. She squeezed his hand tightly and dabbed at her nose. "Yes," she told him. "Of course, the Sunday comics."

"Well," he said. "When I was a little kid, I used to put my nose right up to them. And I was just amazed because it all looked like this mass of dots, and none of it made any sense until I pulled back. Life looks like that mass of dots to me sometimes. None of it makes any sense. But I like to think that, from God's perspective, life, everything—even this—makes sense. It's not just dots. Instead we're all connected, and it's beautiful and funny and good. This close"—he held up an imaginary paper—"we can't expect it to make sense. Not right now."

Lila stood at the open door of her convertible in the hospice parking lot. She extended Aaron's handkerchief, then paused to eye the soggy damage, looking up at him with graceful chagrin. "Thank you," she said.

"Please, keep it," said Aaron.

She smiled bravely. "Thank you. I don't often lose my composure, but when I do, I do."

"Don't worry," he told her. "I'd say it was pretty justified."

Lila took out a small leather business card holder and extracted one of her cards. "Would you please come visit me sometime—at my restaurant? Do say yes. The drinks are on the house."

Aaron studied the card for a moment. "Oh," he said, smiling. "Um…we don't drink."

"Well, that must make your church a bit of a hard sell."

"At times, yes."

"Just hang on to that anyway. Come in for a meal then, or whatever you like."

"OK, ma'am. I will."

"Promise?"

"I promise."

Aaron waited for her to get into the car, then he gently closed the door for her and watched her drive away.

Slowly, happily, he wandered back to his bike and pushed it across the grounds to find Ryder leaning with one hand on the tree.

"So, did you enjoy yourself, talking to the crying lady?"

"Yeah," said Aaron. "I did, actually."

"Good, because we missed lunch."

Misty Johnson

When Ryder got home from his first date with Misty Johnson, he knelt beside his bed in prayer. It was then that he received the revelation that he and Misty should marry, and he was overcome with such fervor and anticipation that he could hardly sleep. He spent most of the night thumbing through *The Book of Mormon.*

The next morning he called her to tell her the good news, but she wasn't home and, since answering machines made him tongue-tied, he hung up. His day was long and filled with all kinds of church obligations anyway. He resigned himself to the fact that he wouldn't be able to talk to her until the next day.

Monday morning he set out to find her on the university campus. At the student union, he found her studying at a table—a cold bagel and coffee perched next to her, light from the window flooding her exquisitely beautiful face.

"Hey, there, I've been lookin' all over for you. Whoa— is that coffee?"

She looked up from her books and smiled. "Hi. Uh-huh."

Ryder took a seat across from her. "But you're Mormon."

"Sort of."

"Sort of? But prophet clearly states that coffee is against the Word of Wisdom."

Misty stared at him. "And do you know why?"

"Because it's bad for you."

"No, because by the time the Mormons reached Utah they'd been so severely persecuted across the rest of the country that they only trusted to eat and drink things they'd cultivated themselves. Since coffee and tea weren't bumper crops in Utah, the Mormons would've had to import them, but they were too paranoid. And *that* is why Mormons don't drink coffee. I, on the other hand, will take my chances."

"Where'd you hear that bogus story?"

"My father learned it at B.Y.U."

"That doesn't make any sense. Why would they teach that at B.Y.U.?"

"Believe it or not."

"Listen, aside from all of that, I've got something of major importance to tell you."

"What?" She looked at him. Her freckled skin was porcelain-white.

"I spoke with God last night and…"

Misty's face dropped. "Whoa. I really hate to interrupt you here, but…I don't really believe in this whole talking-to-God thing. I mean, maybe I should have told you this when we went out the other night."

"What?" Ryder was afraid his news was being discounted.

Misty touched his arm, and tingles of joy rolled through him. "Would it bother you if I told you that I haven't been to church since I was 13?"

"Well, if it's true…"

Her expression told him that it was.

"But you still believe in the church, right? You still have a testimony that it's the true church?"

"A testimony?" Misty almost choked on her bagel.

"Misty?" Ryder was very solemn now. He felt God telling him this was a delicate matter with which he would need to be very careful. "I prayed last night after our date." He paused, taking Misty's silence for reverence. "And God told me, in no uncertain terms, that you were to be my wife."

"But we've only been out on *one* date."

"I know—that's what makes it so powerful." He paused again. "It's destiny."

She looked at him with confusion.

"But," he continued, "you'll need to start going to church. You'll need to pray and fast and pay your tithing. And gain a testimony."

"Listen, Paul. Let me tell you a little story about my testimony…"

"Misty! Are you *even listening to me*?"

"Yes."

"Because you need to understand this—how flippin' important it is–the Heavenly Father *spoke* to me last night!"

Misty looked askance at the people sitting next to them not four inches away, hoping they had not just heard that, and whispered, "Look, I understand that this happened for you, but…"

"Please just tell me that you get the importance."

"OK, OK. I get the importance. Now will you listen?"

"Oh, for Pete's sake, yes."

"When I was a kid, I went to summer camp with the church one year. I had a lot of Mormon friends and we had a blast there—water fights, swimming, scary stories, marshmallows, skits, the whole bit. Well, on our last night there they held a big meeting and served us all hot apple cider as we gathered around. Then, one by one, each girl went up to give her testimony. Everyone kept track of who had gone…and who hadn't."

Ryder was captivated as she paused to pull a strand of hair from her lips.

"The testimonies were all pretty much like 'I believe the LDS church is the one true church, and that Joseph Smith is the true prophet of God' and so on. They all said the same exact thing."

Ryder chuckled. "Well, they were just kids."

"But it was still obligatory!" she said emphatically. "They don't know *what* to say, but they know they have to say *something*. Anyway, it finally came down to two girls, me and Sarah Eddington—and we just stared at each other. Neither one of us were raised Mormon. And Sarah had pink hair! Finally, after a few minutes, Sarah gave in and went up. And she stood there and said just what everyone else had said." Misty took a gulp of coffee. "Then all eyes were on me."

"Sounds like a lot of pressure," said Ryder.

Misty nodded. "I kept wishing everybody would think I already went. But oh, no—they knew. Finally, after, like, the most painfully silent three minutes, I went up."

Ryder relished the way Misty's eyes sparked with defiance. "What did you say?"

"I said, 'Well, I don't really know about the church being true and all. But I do know I love coming to summer camp and hanging out with all you guys. It's really a lot of fun and I think you're all great people. And that's about it. Amen.'"

Ryder gaped at Misty. "You are one brave girl."

"But that's not the point!"

"Still, I'm sure your teachers believed in you. They knew you'd come to see the light because you aren't a bad person."

"Just because I'm not a bad person doesn't mean I'm going to come around and believe in the Mormon Church."

"Misty," said Ryder. "Maybe you've been a little more honest with yourself than others. Maybe you've chosen to take a path that questions the Prophet. And I think that's good. Because I know that when you come back you'll have truly looked at the options and come to this through good faith and hard work—that you're not just a blind believer like all those other losers. Get it? Your faith'll actually mean something—and I'm sure that's why God picked you out for me." Ryder reached for and held her hand. "Because you're special."

Misty sighed heavily, and the rise and fall of her perfumed cleavage worked its magic.

Ryder went on in a mild swoon. "I'll wait for you, Misty. I want you to explore and do all the questioning you have to do. And I'll be here for you, all along. We can date. And maybe I can get you to come to church a few times. I mean, you *were* at the singles social at the Institution when I met you last week. That must mean something!"

"Oh," said Misty. "But I just wanted to meet some new people. Maybe it was the wrong place to look, but Mormons are so easy to meet. They're so *nice*."

Ryder edged forward in his seat. "You're right, they are. But I'm sure there was more to it than that. You don't go to a Mormon singles gathering without…"

"Right. You're right. And I can see now that I made a mistake."

"No," said Ryder. "You followed your destiny. You didn't really even have a choice that night."

"OK, Paul." Misty stood gathering her books and jamming them into an already teeming L.L. Bean backpack. "Hey, can we talk later? I have to go to class."

Once she'd left, Ryder sat staring at the remains of her bagel and the coffee ring left on the table. Why wasn't anything ever simple? Why did God always have to test him?

That next Sunday, Ryder finished his shower, dried himself quickly, and put on his white terrycloth robe. It was frayed a bit around the collar. He would need a new one before his mission.

He picked up the phone and dialed Misty's number. A groggy voice answered after the fourth ring.

"Misty. Hi. Did I wake you?" he asked amusedly, thinking of her with tousled hair and sleepy eyes.

"Mmm. Hi."

"Would you like to come to church with me today? I could pick you up. Or maybe we could walk together."

"Mmm. I don't think so."

"Please, Misty. It'd be so great to have you there."

"You're sweet, but I was up so late last night. I went to the Roasting Company with some friends…"

Ryder felt deflated. "I wanted you to talk to the bishop with me."

"Today?"

"Yes."

"I can't. Not today anyway. Um, maybe next week, OK?"

"Yeah. Sure. Talk to you later."

"OK. Have fun." Her voice was so sympathetic. So *sweet*. She just needed more time. He was rushing her. He would talk to the bishop himself.

Ryder walked to church underneath his umbrella. He thought about his worn blue suit. He would need new suits for his mission too, and some new shirts and probably shoes. He was melancholy when he reached the church. He wanted Misty with him. There were 10 minutes before sacrament meeting. He went off to find the bishop.

Bishop Anderson was a tall, thin gentleman with very pale skin and a singsong voice. He couldn't have been more than 40. Ryder spotted him near his office, surrounded by his counselors—two even paler men in dark suits with somber and important looks on their faces. Ryder lingered in the hallway, not wanting to interrupt. The three men finally began to relax a bit and initiated handshakes. They dispersed, and Ryder called to the bishop, "Bishop Anderson!"

The bishop wheeled around. "Nice to see you today, my boy." He pivoted quickly to greet the person brushing up behind him.

"Uh, sir?"

The bishop swung around with a raised eyebrow.

"I was hoping maybe we could meet today after church."

"Well, I should have a few minutes. Will it take long?"

"Hopefully not."

"Come by my office around 1:15 then."

"Thank you, sir. I'll be there."

"Fine." They shook hands. Ryder reveled in the new respect he was shown by the members of the priesthood. Ever since he had become an elder, he was one of them, and they would grant him a meeting that day if he asked. It was a powerful feeling.

Exactly at 1:15, Ryder knocked on the bishop's door.

"Come in," yelled a muffled voice. Ryder turned the doorknob and saw the bishop's smiling face.

"Sit down, Elder Ryder! Tell me what's on your mind."

Ryder slowly took his seat, wondering how he would start. He was sure Bishop Anderson would make it clear how he could deal with this Misty situation and have it end happily. But another part of him worried that he'd condemn her—that if the bishop knew about Misty's past and the things she said sometimes, that. . .

"Sir, it's about Misty."

"Is that the girl you met at the singles gathering?"

Ryder nodded.

"Seems like a fine girl—misses church too much."

"Sir, I'm in love with her."

"Nothing wrong with that."

"Well, yes and no."

"I hope you're not going to tell me that the two of you…"

"No! Nothing like that, sir! It's just…"

"Whew. Because that's a real biggie and a real toughie. With you going on your mission, you don't want to be dealing with those kinds of indiscretions."

"No." Ryder sat wondering whether to go through with it. But he didn't know where else to turn.

"Sir. I don't think Misty believes in the church."

Bishop Anderson sighed. He leaned back in his big black chair until Ryder thought he would fall over backward. "Also a biggie and a toughie." There was a long pause. The bishop's fingers were steepled and gently tapping against his lips. "You're not going to want to hear this. But you're a young fellow—and there are many pretty young girls out there who will need a husband in two years, good devout girls. You don't need to be wasting time proselytizing to your own girlfriend. Concentrate on the mission, my boy. Don't worry about girls right now. God will provide."

"But that's my dilemma, sir. God told me I was supposed to marry her."

The bishop's fingers came unsteepled. "We shouldn't make the mistake of thinking we always understand what God is trying to say. That's where those polygamists are always getting into trouble—gives us a bad name."

Ryder pondered this. "So what do I do?"

Bishop Anderson stood to put his jacket on. He gathered some papers together and put them in a file. He placed a book that had some ethereal clouds and filtered sunlight on the cover on top of the file and tidied his desk a bit more. Then he rose and went to the door. "Out of time, my boy. Must go."

"But what do I do?"

Bishop Anderson opened the door. He leaned on the doorknob. "Dump her," he said, and then briskly walked down the fluorescent-lit hallway of orange carpet.

Colors and Whites

Monday is preparation day for all Mormon missionaries. It's the day everyone is expected to take care of things like shopping, laundry, and letter-writing. But when Ryder sneezed a mouthful of orange juice onto the pile of freshly pressed white dress shirts Aaron had folded the day before, Aaron received special permission to take care of the problem during the group study session that Tuesday afternoon.

He had a lot to think about anyway, and he took his time, one by one stuffing into the washer the shirts that had soaked in cold water overnight and all Tuesday morning. First, there was the incident in the bedroom with Christian. He'd be sure not to let anything like that happen again. Aaron felt like he had control of it in his mind. He'd made his peace with God and it would not happen again. Period. His conflict was over whether he should tell his mission president. He knew he should. But he also remembered what happened to Elder Todd, the Post-it prankster. What if they sent him home too? Would his father's position in the church be jeopardized? Aaron knew this was not a good reason to withhold the truth. He just needed a few days to figure out for himself what the whole thing meant. If it meant something serious, he would tell his bishop. But if it was just a moment of temptation, and he had withstood it and was ready to move on…

Besides, was he not a willing servant of God? He'd had the most amazing experience talking to that movie star at the hospice center, a powerful sense that he'd actually accomplished something. God *had* spoken through him. What really shook him, though, was that while he'd been wrapped up in his moment with Lila Montagne—he knew who she was now for sure since she'd given him her business card—there had been nothing he wanted to say about the church.

He could barely stand to acknowledge it, but it was right there, staring him down: In letting go of the church, or at least in forgetting about it, he had done more good and felt closer to God than at any other point so far during his mission…

Aaron's thoughts were not clear. Why did he feel so drawn in by people outside of the church?

Flip-flop sandals ka-slapped heavily across the courtyard and down the steps.

Harmon?

Ryder?

No. It was Christian.

Aaron hurried to stuff the remainder of the shirts into the washing machine. He thrust in the quarters and waited for the water to rise up.

Christian parked right next to him to sort a meager pile of white socks and various spandex bike shorts, including one rainbow-colored pair. Aaron glanced over. None of it even looked dirty to begin with. He felt angry. What was with this ruse?

"Hey," said Christian, as he turned a sock right-side-out. "I've never run into you guys on your way out. You're up that early every day?"

"Pretty much," said Aaron coolly.

"I'll bet you were wondering where I was off to."

"Actually," said Aaron. "I just figure you're always going to the gym."

"No." Christian touched his arm. "I've been volunteering." His eyes met Aaron's meaningfully. "For Project Angel Food."

Aaron stepped away, poured out a capful of detergent, and dumped it in. "That's great," he said, jerking the remaining drops out of the cap. "So what do you want from me? Some sort of merit badge?"

"No…it's just"—Christian floundered—"you know, what you said about me, it's not true."

"Fine!" shouted Aaron. "It's not true. And the world is a better place."

Christian stopped feeding his washer. "Whoa, what'd I do?"

"Nothing," said Aaron.

"Then why do you have to be so mean?"

Aaron looked at him. "You're not volunteering there because of what I said, are you?"

"No," said Christian. "I just thought we could…"

"You thought we could what?" said Aaron. "Hang out? Be best friends? Ride off into the sunset?"

"I don't know," Christian offered desperately. "Everyone seems to think that…everyone seems to treat me like I'm…"

"Like you're perfect," said Aaron.

"Yeah," said Christian. "Maybe, sometimes."

Aaron snorted and screwed the top onto his laundry soap.

"But you're the first person I've met who's made me feel like…"

"Like what?"

"Like that's not enough. You know, like maybe I want to be something more. So, I just thought that…"

"Look, whatever you're thinking…don't." Aaron paused at the bottom of the steps. "We're colors and whites. We don't mix."

With each step he took up the stairwell, Aaron's heart pulled him back. He wanted to drop everything, to turn, to run back and throw himself into Christian's arms. But he didn't. He couldn't.

He'd promised God.

Revelations

Wildfires were sweeping through Southern California, and Ryder's snores had taken on a whole new dimension. Every couple of minutes, for as much as 15 seconds at a time, he'd completely stop breathing. For Aaron, the silence that stretched through the dark, faintly smoke-scented bedroom inspired contradictory feelings. On the one hand, he found himself concerned for Ryder's health. And on the other, he wished that these brief periods of apnea would extend through the remainder of the night.

Aaron stared at the ceiling. That afternoon he had run from the one person who made him feel fully and exhilaratingly alive. But why was that? *Our Father in Heaven, I thank you in the name of your son, Jesus Christ, but is this your way of testing me? If I conquer this vulnerability, will I finally be worthy of you?*

Again, Ryder stopped breathing. Soft footsteps scraped across the courtyard. Muted, laughing male voices filtered in through the latched window. Aaron sat up, propped himself on one arm, and cocked his head. He listened to the jingle of keys, followed by the return of Ryder's snores, and then he stood and tiptoed through the darkness. Tonight he did not delude himself that he was worried about burglars. He peeked through the blinds with only one concern: *Christian?*

Aaron's suspicions were confirmed. Christian was unlocking his front door to let in a sharp-faced guy in a polo shirt and jeans. When the door closed behind them, Aaron crossed the room back to his bed. He fell to his knees with his elbows on the mattress, his hands locked in prayer. His knuckles dug into his forehead as tears of relief ran down his face. *Thank you, Lord, for showing me the truth...*

Christian unlocked his front door.

"Fuck, I gotta piss," whispered his date, a sharp-faced man whose name—if he'd ever heard it at all—had escaped Christian hours ago.

The man scurried into the apartment ahead of him.

"Hallway. First door on the right."

Christian glanced at Aaron's window. *Why can't I stop thinking about him? Did I just see the blinds moving? Am I going crazy?* He heard his date curse and looked in after him. He was on the floor, having just tripped over Julie's rollerblades (that girl was such a slob!) and was looking around now in baffled humiliation. Christian watched with barely amused disinterest as the man picked himself up off the floor and, fumbling with his fly, made a mad dash for the bathroom.

Asshole, thought Christian.

He stepped into his apartment and stood in the dark living room listening to his guest empty his bladder into the toilet. The situation he was in, his hair, his clothes, everything about himself seemed acutely trivial. How had he let his apartment's decor become so fussy? He stood in front of the window with his arms crossed and stared up at the crimson crescent moon hanging in the blue-black sky. He frowned. Even the sky looked overdone.

He tried to see Aaron's window, but from that angle it was obscured by the overhang of another bungalow's roof. He pressed his face up to the glass.

He was still doing this when, coming up from behind him, a pair of arms encircled his waist. Next a deft pair of hands made short work of his belt buckle. A fairly average-size hard-on pressed against the inside seam of his back pocket. Were all these attached to the same warm body? Christian turned to give the man a resigned kiss.

But the man backed away. "I don't kiss," he said.

"No?" said Christian, without much surprise.

Then the man dropped his trousers and went to his knees in front of Christian's fly. He delved in and fished it out quickly. Good, it was hard. Even better, it was big.

Christian felt himself slide into pleasure—but then a sudden jolt of anxiety. "What was your name again?"

"Dhhhmmkkk," said the man.

"Dick?"

The man pulled his mouth from the task at hand. He looked up, faintly exasperated. "Dirk."

"Dirk?" said Christian. "Your parents named you Dirk?"

Dirk sat back on his heels. "It's really Mort." He wriggled his eyebrows. "My friends call me 'Water Sports Mort.'"

Dirk jerked Christian's pants down, spun him around, and buried his nose between his ass-cheeks.

"Oh!" Christian braced himself on the sofa. "O-K.....
Um, look—Dirk—it's not that I don't appreciate what
you're doing back there, but...could we have a little talk?"

Dirk pulled back his head. "Talk? Cool, baby. I'm into
that. Ah, fuck, yeah, I'm your nasty little slut boy."

Christian rolled his eyes.

"I'm your pussy whore. Are you gonna smack Mama's
ass? 'Cause she's been a bad, bad girl!" He slapped
Christian hard on the rump.

"Uh, Dirk?"

"Yeah, Daddy?"

"That's not exactly it...I mean, that's not what I
meant." He pivoted around, and bent to pull up his jeans.
"I meant"—he pulled Dirk up off his knees and to his
feet—"I meant conversation."

"Conversation?" said Dirk. "Why?"

Christian stared at him. "Don't you ever want to get to
know someone? Have it mean something? Maybe sleep
with a guy, and actually *sleep* with him?"

"You want to what?" Dirk looked puzzled. "Sleep
together? I don't know, man. Isn't that kind of...intimate?"

"Excuse me," Christian laughed, fastening his jeans,
"but a moment ago you were licking my spleen. Sleeping
with me would be too intimate?"

Dirk stared at Christian like he'd just seen a ghost. He
lifted his hands in surrender. "OK, now you're really starting to freak me out. I'm just gonna go, man. I didn't know
you were into weird shit." He grabbed his polo shirt, backed
away with it slowly, then turned and sprinted for the door.

Keith

When Keith first suspected he was HIV-positive, it was a beautiful spring afternoon. He was lying in bed, having just had some of the best sex of his life with a guy who'd been a military spacecraft fighter—eye-candy, basically—in one of those wildly popular alien soul-sucker movies back in the '80s. Poor R. hadn't had many lines and was killed within the first 30 minutes, but Keith had remembered him for years after seeing the movie, and he was psyched to be in bed with him, when his phone rang. "Mr. Griffin, it's Teresa from the family clinic," said the young nurse's aide on the line. "Mr. Griffin, you need to come down to the clinic as soon as possible. I need to talk to you about your result."

"So I have a result?" asked Keith.

"I just need you to come down to the clinic," said Teresa. "Can you come now?"

"Can you tell me whether I have a result?"

"I'm sorry, I just need you to come to the clinic."

Keith hung up the phone and lay for a moment in silence. Space warrior was sleeping next to him, his dark skin catching the light from the window. He looked so peaceful. Keith got up, pulled a shirt and some shorts on, stepped into some flip-flops, and walked out the front door. He got in his car and drove to the clinic.

He had never even meant to have an HIV test. He was the kind of guy who was too busy and didn't want to know anyway, but he'd come down with a persistent rash, and as he was having it checked, in an unpredictable moment of responsibility, he asked the doctor. Almost as if he wanted to show the doctor how responsible he was. He never intended to get the results. He never even thought about it after that.

But when he got the call, in an instant he knew he was positive. On his way to the clinic he began to dissociate himself from the world. *There's a line now,* he decided. *Between me and everyone else not positive.* He began to see his life in finite terms, as something with a beginning, a middle, and an end. He experienced probably a dozen shifts in perspective on the way to clinic, which was only a 15-minute drive.

It was not the most reputable of clinics he had gone to, just a clinic headquarters his insurance carrier had a low-cost arrangement with, a shoddy building in Silver Lake he sometimes visited for things he was too embarrassed to see his regular doctor about. The fact that it was not upscale may have been what made him comfortable asking for a test to begin with. With his regular doctor, he felt too despicable. Here, surrounded by the poor, he felt almost like he couldn't be touched by HIV. And he also felt that if he were to learn he was positive, it should be in a place like this.

Keith checked in and sat in the waiting room. They were showing a videotape about a pets program for people with AIDS. Keith watched the video in a cold sweat. It was the last thing he wanted to see.

When they called him in, he waited in the small office until the nurse's aide, Teresa, came in. Teresa had taken his initial blood sample. Was she looking at him funny? She was. "OK, Mr. Griffin. I have to tell you something, and I hope you won't be mad at me. When I took your blood the other day, I took the wrong kind of sample."

"Huh?"

"I put the sample into two test tubes, which are the size for another kind of test. Because I sent the wrong type of sample to the lab, they were unable to perform the test…"

Keith listened as the aide rambled on about her mistake. So he didn't have HIV? The nurse's aide had called him in just to take a new sample? She was begging him not to tell her supervisor because she didn't want to lose her job…?

Keith felt numb. Relieved, yet totally mind-fucked. He looked at the girl. "So, what?" he said. "You just gotta take more blood?"

Two weeks later Keith got a valid result back.

He was positive.

Strategy Versus Fate

Pfff-sss, pfff-sss.

Keith dozed in his chair in the dark, tomb-like living room. He'd fallen asleep with his headphones on, listening to a Bach symphony concerto on his CD player, and was dreaming now that he was in a crowded rest room where lovely young men lined up to have sex. One did a line of crystal meth on the sink before approaching him. "Let's do it without a condom," he said.

"I'm positive," said Keith.

"I don't care...I'm on my way out anyway."

Keith cringed.

"Please," said the young man.

A knock at the door—someone was coming in.

He opened one eye to see Christian standing in the archway with the usual food delivery bag. Today he was dressed like a Benetton model posing as pizza delivery boy: yellow T-shirt, jeans, white leather Converse, and backward-facing baseball cap. Keith groaned. He was as hatefully beautiful as last time.

"Oh," said Keith. He peeled away his headphones. "It's back."

"Yeah, it's back." Christian strode over to the piano and set the food bag down on top of the debris. "This must be your lucky fuckin' day."

Keith sniffed. "Or maybe I'm just not suffering enough yet. I didn't expect to see you again."

Christian opened the bag and pulled out a hot foil container with chicken cacciatore and rice. He set it down on a wooden TV tray, and reached back into the bag for an apple. "Oh, come on," he said over his shoulder with his hands propped on his knees. "You don't think your going all 'Miss Cleo the Psychic' on my ass is going to scare me off that easy—now, do you?"

Keith offered up a small smile. "Maybe it was just dementia setting in. Sometimes I read people and I think I'm the oracle at Delphi."

Christian finished up by arranging a few napkins and some plastic silverware next to the meal. "Yeah? Well, sometimes I growl at people, but that doesn't make *me* Eartha Kitt." He pivoted around with the tray, and bent to place it on top of Keith's ottoman. "I'm just going put this…right about…here."

His client looked at him tiredly. "It doesn't matter. I'm still not hungry."

"I don't remember asking you if you were. I just deliver this stuff, remember? But my friend Andrew *made* this, and he doesn't even cook for his boyfriend." Christian moved his face in close. "So the least you could do is try to be polite, and eat it."

Keith stared into his lap. "I don't have to pretend to be polite. I think I've…I think I've earned that right."

"Oh, yes, that's right," said Christian, pulling up a musty but stylish antique chair. "You're dying, you're bitter, blah, blah, blah… Fortunately, I'm shallow, so I'm impervious to that. Now eat it."

"Impervious?" said Keith. "Bet you don't know how to spell that."

"Sure I do," said Christian, switching on a nearby reading lamp. "It's spelled: Bite me." He reached into his back pocket and pulled out a rolled-up tabloid newspaper. "And just to show you that our little problems in this world don't amount to a hill of beans, while you eat, I'm going to read about some people"—he opened up the newspaper—"who have some real trouble."

Christian crossed his ankle over one knee, leaned back in his chair, and disappeared behind the paper. After a long suspenseful moment, during which Keith watched his white leather sneaker wiggling up and down, he gasped. "Oh, my…oh, I can't believe… Say it isn't so."

Keith didn't budge, but his eyebrows shot up. "What?"

Christian folded the paper closed. "Apparently, poor Pam Anderson has had her breast implants taken out and put back in so many times that her entire chest is collapsing." He reopened the paper, his pupils dilating. "Oh, my God," he squealed, "they have bikini pictures!" He bent in the top corner of the paper and entertained Keith with a scandalized expression. "They're horrible."

"Shut up," said Keith.

"No, they are—seriously. They're down to her knees." He smiled slyly. "Eat your chicken and I'll show you."

Keith edged over, but Christian leaned away from him and pressed the photos to his chest. "Ah, ah, ah—take a bite first."

Keith sank into his chair in a complete sulk. Churlishly, he folded his bony arms over his distended little gut and crossed his legs. But resistance was futile, and they both knew it. Seconds passed. Keith stared at the ceiling, and swallowed. His mouth felt dry. Oh, how he thirsted for just a sip of that catty gossip. He uncrossed his arms. He gripped the armrests of his chair as if ready to heave himself to his feet. But he didn't.

Instead he just slowly reached for his fork.

"Prick," he said, narrowing his eyes at Christian. "OK, give me the fuckin' magazine."

The evening sky was a deep murky violet. Christian pulled his red RAV4 to the curb and hopped out, humming the theme from *Rocky*. He jabbed. He danced. He held his arms over his head. He had gotten Keith to eat that morning, and he still felt like a superstar. He shadowboxed up the front steps, crossed the courtyard to his mailbox, and found no mail, but a note inside.

Christian—
Went to Malibu for a few days. Mom's freaked out about the fires and needs some company. Wanna come? Please?
Julie

As Christian stood reading the note, he heard the *tick-tick-tick* of a spinning bicycle wheel. He turned to see Aaron cresting a bike over the top of the steps with another bike—its front wheel bent at a wicked angle—slung over his shoulder. He looked dazed and scared. His hair was messed up, his shirt untucked on one side.

"Whoa, whoa, whoa." Christian dropped the note and

rushed over to help him. "Aaron, what happened?"

Aaron let him take the mangled bike from his shoulder. He leaned on the other bike and cupped his forehead. "There was an accident. Ryder and I were tracting, but th-there was this car…and it had to be going, well, it was going way too fast."

"Hold on," said Christian. He stood the bike up against the apartment, then took the other one and did the same.

Aaron looked on in a state of shock.

"You OK?" asked Christian.

"I don't know," said Aaron. "I…"

"Never mind, let's get you inside."

Aaron climbed onto his porch. "I swerved," he said as he fumbled with his keys. "And he still hit me…"

"Here," said Christian, taking the keys from him and unlocking the door. He put his hand on Aaron's waist and ushered him in.

"I wiped out in the gutter," said Aaron, staggering into the living room. He slipped off his shoulder bag and set it down on the floor. "But I was lucky…I came out of it with only a few scrapes. But Ryder…" He was pacing. "He went down hard. Hit his head. He either dislocated or broke his shoulder. It looked bad, like it was"—he gulped—"out of the socket. And…and he was just lying there, and they took him to the hospital. I wish I could've warned him. Harmon and Gilford are there now. The ER doctor said he could have a concussion and they might have to keep him overnight. I came back to get his stuff." He struck his forehead with his fists. "I should have warned him."

"No, no, no, don't say that." Christian gently pulled Aaron's fists down and put a comforting hand on his shoulder. "Accidents happen."

"But I was th-th-thinking about…" stuttered Aaron, "I wasn't p-paying attention because…" He stood, frozen, his eyes trained on Christian's hand, which looked so loving just resting there on his shoulder. It was like he was watching a movie. And the film had slowed down to show how meaningful the moment was.

Christian followed Aaron's gaze to where it rested on his hand. Suddenly he was conscious of the intimacy between them. *It's like we're in a prism,* he thought. *A beautiful prism of light and comfort and…*

Aaron surrendered as Christian pulled him into his arms. Their bodies melded together. Aaron told him, "I was thinking about you."

"Shhh." Christian stroked the back of his head. "Everything's going to be OK."

Aaron clutched him tighter. He brushed his lips across the smooth skin of Christian's cheek.

Suddenly, Christian pulled away. "Look," he said. "You're in no position, so I should just…go."

And then their eyes locked. And Christian knew that no matter what the circumstances were, Aaron did not, would not want him to ever go. He slowly reached up to caress Aaron's cheekbone with his thumb. Their faces moved closer. Their noses, then their lips touched. The world stopped, and Christian again experienced the sense of being floated inside a prism, a prism filled only with their breath, and their racing hearts, and their kiss. It was like the room was circling them, as if the entire universe had broken apart and heaven had been laid wide open…

"Ah, for flippin' gross," came a voice from the doorway.

"Pretty boy's not the only fag around here."

Ryder stood in the open doorway with his left arm in a sling and a thick piece of gauze taped to his forehead. Harmon and Gilford were positioned behind him, glaring menacingly over his shoulder like hired thugs.

Aaron winced and turned his back on them. Christian stepped in front of him protectively. "OK, look," he said. "Nothing happened here."

Ryder hobbled in closer, focusing his eyes on the two of them shrewdly. "We walked in here and you two were mackin' like schoolgirls and you're saying nothing happened?"

"Schoolgirls?" said Christian. "I don't know what kind of schools they have in Utah, but maybe you should try to reach down into your little Bible-geek soul and try to be cool for two seconds."

Ryder moved up into Christian's face and planted a hard finger on his chest. "I don't think you get to be making any requests here"—he shoved him backward—"gay boy."

Christian smacked Ryder's hand away. "Don't fucking touch me, asshole."

Gilford stepped in between the two of them, putting a heavy hand on Christian's shoulder. "Dude," he said huskily. "You sooo gotta be leaving right now."

Christian walked past him to the doorway. "Look, you guys, don't blow this out of proportion. It's no big deal." He turned to Aaron for confirmation. "Right?"

"Yeah. It is, kind of." Aaron could not bring his eyes from the floor. "Please—could you just go?"

"You heard the man," said Gilford.

Christian walked out of the apartment. Crossing the courtyard, he kicked the wheel of Ryder's bike so viciously that it slammed to the ground. He ran, leapt down the steps to the sidewalk, sprinted for his SUV, and got in. Breathing hard, he switched on the ignition, and peeled away from the curb.

Julie and Traci were already up in Malibu enjoying the relaxed environment of Julie's mom's beach house and her hospitality, which always included a hot Jacuzzi bath in Marla's sunken concrete tub, followed by a tarot card reading, and then the selection of whatever DVD looked good from the library. Lounging in the family room in terrycloth robes, they were partly through their second Bridget Fonda movie and a third tub of microwave popcorn when Christian pounded on the door.

"Julie," said Marla, a lovely slight-framed woman in her mid-40s who, after a fairly lucrative soap opera career and an even more lucrative divorce, had chosen to live far from the glamour of Hollywood. She wore threadbare jeans and an embroidered hemp hippie-smock, with enough face powder, lipstick, and mascara to be appropriately made-up for an awards banquet. Her manicure was impeccable. "Your friend Christian is here."

"You came!" shouted Julie excitedly. "Hey, get in here—we're watching *Single White Female* and Traci keeps skipping back to the part where Jennifer Jason Leigh kills the boyfriend with her stiletto heel…hey, what's wrong?"

"Yeah, what's wrong?" said Traci, from her spot on the sofa. "You look terrible."

"I just did something stupid," said Christian. "I got someone in trouble."

Julie frowned. "What? Who?"

"Aaron," he said. "I think I just got him kicked out of the church."

Marla put her arm around Christian and guided him to the kitchen. "Honey, come in here and sit down. Let me get you some Zen tea."

Having slept in his clothes the night before and driven back from Malibu late the next morning, Christian dragged himself out of his car and up the steps to the courtyard. Somebody had put Ryder's bike away, but the shrubs were still broken and bedraggled in the spot where it had landed. Christian seethed, remembering what an asshole Ryder had been. He walked to the front porch of bungalow 3D, went up the steps, and knocked loudly. Some shuffling occurred behind the door, and when it finally swung open, there, with one hand resting on the doorknob, was a missionary he'd never seen before—a stocky, red-haired youth in a short-sleeve white shirt that was buttoned up to the collar, navy trousers, and periwinkle blue socks. The youth stood blinking inquisitively at Christian with a set of eyes that were too close together, and no apparent eyebrows.

"Um, hi," said Christian, craning his neck to see past the new missionary. The elders' butt-ugly sofa was gone and packed-up boxes covered the floor. "I was looking for Aa—I mean, is Elder Davis around?"

"Too late, loverboy." Ryder appeared at the far end of

the living room, still hampered by the sling on his left arm. He made his way over to the doorway, stumbling over boxes and booting one of the beanbag chairs aside. "You'd better betcha they're putting your boyfriend's butt on a plane home this afternoon. And we have to move again because we can't live across from a big doodah flamer homo." The redheaded missionary was still politely holding the door open. Ryder stepped ahead of him to confront Christian. He cocked his head sarcastically. "Thank you very much."

Christian jerked his hand across the threshold, latched on to the front of Ryder's shirt, and hauled him out onto the porch.

"Ack!" squawked Ryder.

Christian pointed a serious finger at the new guy, who seemed to observe with relative calm the fact that his new missionary companion had just been put in a chokehold. "You stay," Christian said firmly. "Your friend and I are going to have a little talk."

The new kid nodded.

Christian dragged Ryder to the far end of the courtyard. He shoved his back up against the wall. "OK, asshole, the way I see it, you've got a big mouth and only one arm to back it up." Ryder used his one good arm to hit Christian in the ear with a sharp right hook. When Christian relaxed his grip, Ryder made a break for it, but Christian regained his hold and thrust him back even harder against the wall, then jostled his hurt shoulder for good measure.

"Ow! Hey!"

"How's it going to look when a big flamer kicks the shit out of you?" He lifted the slight young missionary by the straps of his sling so that he came up on his toes. "Ryder! I'm not fucking around. Just tell me where he is!"

"What?" shouted Ryder. "Do you think I wanted to see him get busted?" He clawed at Christian's wrist. "This may come as a surprise to you, but I actually liked the guy. He took this whole mission thing as serious as a seizure, but we were actually getting through it OK."

Christian loosened his grip.

"So," said Ryder angrily. "Why him, huh?" He lowered his voice. "Why'd you have to go fuck him up? He doesn't deserve the kind of grief he's got coming down the pike."

Subdued by his own guilt, Christian let go of him. "Hey, look, nothing was supposed to happen to him. It was just…"

"Bullpucky," spat Ryder. "You were gunning for something ever since we got here. You don't think I noticed you making eyes at him all the time and…and running down to the laundry room every time he was in there. Now, if you want to know where he is, I want to know why."

Christian's eyes met Ryder's.

"You heard me," said Ryder. "The whole story…or you get nothing."

Christian stumbled over his story. "It was…stupid. At first it was—it was just a dumb bet—50 bucks."

Ryder couldn't believe it. He was disgusted.

"Wait," said Christian. "But it's not about that now. It's not about that at all."

Ryder stared at him. "And you expect me to care?"

"Please," Christian said. "I'm begging you."

Ryder checked his watch. "You're too late anyway. His flight left 10 minutes ago."

Christian swallowed hard, defeated. He turned away.

Ryder watched him. He thought of Misty. "Hey."

Christian turned. Ryder stepped forward tentatively. "Look, if it's any help, his flight has a five-hour layover in Salt Lake."

Christian's eyes filled with hope—then gratitude. "Thanks."

Ryder shrugged.

Snow

A plane touched down in an early winter snowstorm.

"Welcome to Salt Lake City," said the stewardess over the intercom system.

Christian unfastened his safety belt and began to make his way toward the front of the plane. He felt a firm tug on the back of his shirt. He stopped, whipped around. A tiny stewardess gripped his wrist. Her dogged expression frightened him. "Sir, please sit down and refasten your safety belt until the captain has shut off the 'fasten seat-belt' sign." Christian looked over his shoulder. If he didn't get to the front of the plane before the other passengers filed out of their seats, he'd waste valuable seconds. He considered breaking free and running, but her little grip was so sure that he felt positive she knew judo.

He looked at her. "My wife is having a baby," he said. "I need to be at the hospital. Can I please just wait at the front of the plane?"

"I'm sorry, but it isn't safe to move about the cabin while we're still taxiing—especially in these weather conditions—so *sir*, please sit down," said the stewardess. "And fasten your safety belt."

Christian returned to his seat.

The stewardess winked at him as he fastened his belt.

"Once the plane stops, I'll hold everyone until you can get off." Then she leaned down and whispered in his ear, "But if you think I'm buying the whole 'my wife is having a baby story,' you've got another thing coming, sister."

The stewardess was true to her word. She made everyone stay seated, citing a "medical emergency," while Christian rushed off the plane and hit the exit tunnel full-tilt. He emerged into a sea of white people. Uh-oh. How was he supposed to find Aaron in this crowd? He looked around. No sign of him. He stared at the monitor, scanning Southwest airline flights to Pocatello. There were three. He memorized the gate numbers.

After visiting all three gates, with no sign of Aaron anywhere, Christian began to doubt his decision. He'd just doubled his credit card debt, and for what? What if Ryder lied? Damn—of all people to trust. Just then he saw Aaron walking away from him down the corridor. He rushed up, grabbed his arm. "Aaron—oh...sorry." The young man who slowly pivoted around had a completely different face.

Christian wandered the corridors, wondering what to do next. Should he check the bathrooms? He rushed down another corridor on the way the nearest men's room, passing a set of glass doors that led to a smoking patio. Christian stopped, backed up, and pressed his forehead to the glass.

A lone figure—with no jacket—stood on the patio. Snow came down in flurries all around him. It was Aaron. *What's he doing out there?* wondered Christian. *It's gotta be fucking freezing.*

Aaron took off his name-tag, studied it for a moment, running his fingers over the engraved words, then tossed it Frisbee-style into the trash, raising his arm like a matador in an angry yet remorseful gesture. Slowly the arm came down. Aaron buried his hands in his pockets and stared down at his shoes. When he looked up, he saw Christian on the other side of the door.

Christian walked outside. "God, I hate the snow."

Aaron looked at him. "What are you doing here?"

The snow picked up, dusting them with great white clumps. Steam came from their mouths as they spoke.

"I came after you. How could you just leave without saying anything?"

Aaron shivered. "It's not my choice. I am being sent home in shame. And I'm probably going to be excommunicated."

"For a kiss?" said Christian. "I mean, it *was* a very nice kiss, but come on. We didn't even get to use our tongues."

"You wouldn't understand," said Aaron. "My life is ruined, and you're acting like I've stood you up for the prom."

"I'm sorry," said Christian. He hugged himself to keep warm. "I'm not very good at this. See, I've never made a fool out of myself for anyone before. I've certainly never chased anyone across two states." He stared into Aaron's eyes. "But I've also never felt this way about anyone in my entire life."

Aaron shook his head, smiling skeptically. "What if I'm just some guy you can't have? And then next week you'll be on to your next conquest?"

"And what if you're not?" Christian shouted. "Huh? What if everything in my entire pathetic life, which I happen to love, has led me to this point? Right here, right now. What if you're the blinding light in the middle of the road that strikes me like that guy, the guy in—"

"The Bible?" said Aaron.

"Yeah."

"Paul?"

"*Yeah*. And what if everything has changed like that...and lions lay down with lambs and colors mix with whites? What if you're the one that I've been waiting for my whole life and I let you go?"

"And what if I'm not?" said Aaron. "You have no idea what I'd be giving up."

"Damn it! What is wrong with you? You want revelations engraved in gold and angels trumpeting down from heaven? But what if this is it instead? Me, telling you I love you, right here, in the snow?" Christian's eyes grew damp. He set his jaw. "I love you, Aaron—and I feel like that's pretty miraculous. But if you don't feel the same, I'll go. I'll walk, and you can pretend that this was just some coincidence. You can pretend there wasn't some reason that we met, and that you're sorry I ever walked into your life."

Christian turned. Like a defeated prizefighter, he stalked through the blowing white to the door. Aaron watched him, his face a mask of pain, his lips moving in silent prayer...*turn around, turn around.*

Christian pulled at the doors. But they were locked. He jerked at them viciously. Nothing. His eyes landed on a yellow sticker posted just above the handles: THESE DOORS ARE

TO REMAIN UNLOCKED DURING BUSINESS HOURS. He tugged again—but the doors still refused to budge. He wheeled around, freezing, and desperate to find another way inside. He passed a stunned Aaron. "God, I hate the snow."

Aaron grabbed his arm, held him up, moved in, and kissed him hard. It was a kiss that communicated all the pent-up desire in his soul.

"Whoa," said Christian as they finally backed away from each other. "Now, that one had some tongue."

"Hello," called a man's voice. "You two fellas OK?"

They sought out and located the janitor, a red-faced man whose chest hairs sprouted out above the zipper of his royal-blue jumpsuit. He was grinning as he held open one of the glass doors. "These darn things are always freezing shut. But, hey, you gotta be smarter than the ice, right? I just use my lighter to melt 'em apart again. You boys come in before you freeze too."

Christian and Aaron stumbled toward the bearlike man.

"Come on," he told them. "They're closing the whole airport on account of this storm."

Jeremy Cook had been a clerk at the Salt Lake Airport Inn for three years and was pretty sure he could size up a couple right quick. Pulling a ballpoint pen from the pocket of his maroon blazer, he checked and rechecked the register. "I'm very sorry about this," he said, rubbing a finger over his chapped lower lip. "But what with the storm and all, we're about full up. We're clean out of doubles. You two fellas mind sharing one king-size bed?"

Christian regarded Aaron. "I'm OK, if you're OK."

"I'm OK," said Aaron, shrugging.

SLAM! Barely had they closed the door when Aaron fell upon Christian. He pinned him against the wall and kissed him heatedly. Aaron ripped his tie loose as Christian unbuttoned his shirt for him and tugged it off over his head. Aaron kicked off his shoes, jerked down his trousers, and shucked them to the wall. He pulled back, standing in front of Christian in his very ordinary-looking long underwear, suddenly self-conscious, suddenly aware of what this moment meant.

Then, like a man diving into cold water, he sucked in a deep breath and just went with it. He reached behind his head to between his shoulder blades, grabbed the fabric of his shirt, and whipped it off.

Later the two lounged naked amid twisted sheets. Their bodies—gleaming like burnished sculpture—were upside-down in the bed. "Wow," said Christian as he stroked Aaron's sweat-soaked hair. "How long were we at it?"

Aaron rolled over and reached beyond the foot of the bed for his pants. He retrieved his silver watch from the front left pocket, flipped it open, and studied it. "Two and a half hours." He looked at Christian for approval. "That's OK, right?"

Christian laughed, hugging him. "OK? That's amazing."

Aaron blushed. "I don't know how long you're supposed to do it, ya know?"

"Hey," said Christian. "Is that a real pocket watch?"

"Yeah, dumb, huh?"

"No, why would I think it was dumb? Let me see it."

Christian gently took the watch. " It's cool. How old is it?"

"It was actually my great grandfather's, and he gave it to my grandfather when he was a missionary and my grandfather gave it to my father when he went on his mission. And he gave it to me…" Aaron took the watch back and stared cockily into Christian's eyes. "But I don't think you came here for a genealogy lecture." He flipped it to the floor and pounced, licking his new lover's collarbone, his nipple, and down his quaking abs to… "What's wrong?" he asked, laughing. "What's so funny?"

"Nothing," laughed Christian. "You know, I guess I just sort of thought you'd be a little more reticent…"

"Oh?"

"Yeah, but it's kind of a pleasant surprise."

Aaron lifted his head. "Well, since I'm already going to hell for kissing you, I may as well take the scenic route." He tried to smile, but his lip trembled. "Yup, aside from murder, this is about the worst thing I can do. And given the choice, my family would probably rather I killed someone."

"You're serious?"

Aaron nodded.

"What kind of God do you people believe in?"

Aaron sat up and stared at the wall. "It's not just God," he said finally. "It's everything. It's my family. It's all my friends. It's most of my high school class, my hometown, everything I've known." He reached over to stroke Christian's jaw. "This, you, tonight—I'm turning my back on it all. But, you know"—he smacked Christian's chest with bittersweet affection—"I guess a guy like you can't really understand what that's like…to be completely cut off ."

Christian grabbed Aaron's hand and stared up at the ceiling. An icy wind roared through the parking lot. His voice, when it came, was remote. "When I was 13, my dad... He was this macho, hotshot banker guy." Christian sat up. "And I was this skinny kid who had been caught trying on his mom's shoes one too many times." He paused, kissing Aaron softly on the shoulder. "Anyway, my dad said he'd rather die than raise a little nellie-boy—and I thought I'd rather die than be one. So my dad, who had never even been out of the city in his entire life, decided we were going to go hunt deer.

"So dear old dad—he dragged me to this lodge up in the Sierras. And it was our last day, and I still hadn't shot anything. It was early November, same as now, and there was this storm that came rolling in, but my dad was so determined that his sissy boy was going to kill something, he wouldn't let us leave.

"The snow came in at us from all sides until everything— the sky, the ground, the air—was all the same horrible, screaming white. And I thought, *We're gonna be OK, right?* And I really believed we would be, until I saw my father's eyes...and they were that same white." Christian's jaw was taut. His brow was beaded with sweat.

"And that's when he did it."

"What?" said Aaron. "He did what?"

"Ran...he ran," said Christian, shutting his eyes tightly like he still couldn't believe it. "And I tried to keep up, but there was this jagged branch, and I tripped and tumbled down into this creek bed. And I lost my gun and cut my arm." Christian traced a finger down the inside of his biceps. "That's how I got this scar."

Aaron touched the scar with his finger.

"And when I climbed out, I was covered in snow and I was bleeding and I was alone."

"He didn't"—Aaron swallowed—"come back?"

"No," answered Christian. "He didn't. I've heard people say that when you freeze to death, it's almost pleasant. But it's not—it's excruciating. But I did get calm after a while. I knew I was going to die. That's when I heard it. I heard an angel singing."

Aaron looked at him. "An angel?" he said softly.

"It was so cold, and I was so tired, and I thought, OK, let's just get this over with. So I staggered over to where the angel was singing—and it turned out not to be an angel."

"What was it?"

"Just the wind over some rocks—a cave opening. Once I crawled inside at least I was out of the snow, and I guess I drifted off. When I woke up it was dark. It was still snowing hard. And then I heard this sort of growling noise at the mouth of the cave."

"Growling?" said Aaron.

"Yeah, like a bear," said Christian. "And it reached into the cave and it grabbed me and I tried to fight, but I was so weak and cold that all I could do was"—he paused, ruffling Aaron's hair—"knock the bear's hood off."

"The bear had a hood?"

"Well, it turned out to be a bear only in the sense that the Search and Rescue guy was pretty hairy. But that's when things got weird."

"Not until then?"

"He ripped off all my clothes," said Christian. "And then he tore all his clothes off."

Aaron laughed. "Are you sure you weren't delirious?"

"No, I'm positive it happened that way. Then he stuffed us both into a sleeping bag."

"Oh, wait," said Aaron. "That's the treatment for hypothermia. I remember from the Boy Scout manual."

"Exactly. But I didn't know what to think. I was just so tired and cold and scared." Christian smirked to himself, then he met Aaron's eyes. "But in spite of it all, I popped the biggest woody ever."

"Ha!" laughed Aaron.

"And he just wrapped those big arms around me and pulled me into that hairy chest and told me I was going to be OK. It was the first moment in the whole ordeal that I began to cry."

"I don't blame you," said Aaron. "I would have been freaked out too."

"No," said Christian. "It was joy. I had thought I'd rather die than be gay. I'd gotten a pretty good idea of what dying felt like, but lying there in the arms of that man, I thought, if this is what being gay feels like, bring it on."

Aaron pressed his forehead into Christian's, reconsidering his assumptions, and—as if he really believed he could reconcile this—kissed him passionately.

Christian woke up the next morning amid rumpled sheets. He flipped over to throw an arm across Aaron, but there was no one there. What? He got up and walked to the tiny hotel bathroom. The toilet was busted and was running on continual flush. But no Aaron. He felt a heavy thud in his stomach. Why? He went back to the bed, convincing himself that he had just missed something. But, no—Aaron was gone. The only remaining sign of him was a strand of hair and a shallow dent left in the pillow. Christian drew in a shaky breath. His eyes caught on a sharp glint of light at the floor near the bed-skirt. He crouched down and saw that it was the end of a chain. He pinched it between his fingers and drew out Aaron's antique pocket watch.

Christian flipped the watch shut, clenched it in his fist, and brought it slowly to his lips.

Pocatello Airport

What would she tell people?

How would she explain it to the women in her knitting group?

Gladys Davis sat alone at the end of a long row of chairs inside the terminal, with a warm coat on her lap and her purse jammed under one arm. The cold November sun shone through the window like a spotlight in her eyes. She shut them tight and hunched her shoulders, wishing she could simply disappear.

Aaron stared at her from a short distance, having just exited the tunnel. Her posture was withdrawn. There were dark circles under her eyes. Her orange hair was barely combed, her barrettes—hurriedly applied after an argument with his father—were uneven. It pierced his heart to know that he was responsible for this.

He approached her with words of love and apology running through his mind, but when she opened her eyes and saw him he was shocked. Her face at first softened with concern, but then it hardened into resentment. She stood, took a few steps forward, and extended his wool coat to him in shameful silence. With her eyes averted, she held it out, bending forward, nearly locking her elbows, and tilting back her head, intent on maintaining as much distance as possible. She slunk away as soon as he took it from her.

Aaron had imagined all kinds of scenarios at the airport. His enraged father demanding the return of his sacred garments, his pocket watch, his Bible. A crowd of hecklers with signs reading FAGS BURN IN HELL. Even a torch-bearing lynch mob. But he had not imagined the agony of this simplest thing: the rejection of his own mother.

Making no attempt to close the space between them, he watched her dig around in her purse for her keys. When she finally located them and pulled them out, she walked off ahead of him. "Come on," she said. "Let's get you home."

"Mom," he called after her.

She stopped, but did not turn around. "What, Aaron?"

"I still have to get my luggage."

"Then get it," she said. "I'll meet you out at the car."

Bursting in on the tension, a sugary voice lilted from across the terminal. "Gladys? Why Gladys Davis, I *thought* that was you."

Gladys turned, her face falling as she recognized Noreen Douglas, a whippet of a woman with a shock of lacquered brown curls.

"I was just putting John's mom on the plane for Denver," Noreen said, scurrying up as she wrung the hem of her kitten-embroidered sweater. "Her sister's having problems, bless her heart. Apparently, she's got some kidney stones the size of kumquats. I don't even know what a kumquat is, but it don't sound like something I'd like to try peein' out."

"No," said Gladys nervously. "I don't imagine so… well, I have to be…"

"Oh, Aaron. My stars!" Noreen had tracked the direction of Gladys's nervous glance. "I didn't even notice you standing way over there. Didn't we just send you off a couple of months ago?"—she threw a hand to her mouth, suddenly remembering a fresh bit of gossip—"oh."

Noreen had hit the brakes with all the subtlety of a Mack truck.

Gladys gave her a look.

"Well…" said Noreen. "I best get to getting. I've got to pick up Didi at the dentist—she's got this thing with her braces. Nice to see you both."

Gladys sighed, staring out the window at the ugly half-melted snow. She dug in her purse, then realized she already had the keys in her hand. She smiled, not exactly at Aaron, but at something over his shoulder—tight lips, no teeth. "Go on, go get your luggage and let's get you home before the rest of the world gets to gawk at you."

Lounging in her favorite green T-shirt, Julie sat in front of the window at the kitchen table, absently plucking the strings of her acoustic guitar, which warmed her lap like a giant companionable dog. It was a lonely, gray morning—perfect for turning out something melancholy. Here and there, she'd pause to take a sip of coffee or to pick up a pen and scribble a few lines into her notebook. Just then, from its easy-access position on the table, the phone rang.

Julie answered it. "Hello?"

"Hello? Julie Taylor?"

"Yes?"

"Hi, Julie. Clive Davis here…"

"Very funny. Fuck you, Andrew." Julie punched the hang-up button and clapped the phone back onto the table just as Christian dragged himself through the front door. He dropped his bag in the entryway.

She looked at him. His clothes looked like he'd been sleeping on the street for two days. His hair was plastered to his head. His eyes were swollen, his face gray.

"Where the hell have you been?"

"Salt Lake City," said Christian.

"What?"

Christian walked to the table and began to sort through the mail. "I went after Aaron."

"Wait a minute." Julie set down her guitar. "If you hauled your ass all that way you better tell me you won the bet."

Christian sighed. "I think I'm the loser on this one." He wandered off in the direction of the kitchen. "Man, I need some coffee."

"Hey," said Julie, grabbing his hand. "Don't let it get to you. Even Tiger Woods slices every now and then."

"Julie, please. He meant something to me. OK?"

"What? Oh, my God, Christian, I didn't mean to be…oh, my God, come here." She stood to give him a hug.

The phone rang again. Julie turned, picked it up, pushed ANSWER, then jammed both thumbs on the END button. She slammed it down on the table. "Fucking Andrew!"

Christian laughed, his morning breath wafting away from him like a cloud of poisonous gas. "What? Is he doing his 'Crackhead Telemarketer' again?"

"No, he's jerking me around by..." She stopped, rethinking it for a moment. "Christian?" she said, poking his chest with her finger. "On the off chance...you didn't happen to give my demo to anyone, did you?"

"Uh, yeah. This Angel Food guy I deliver to. He said he was once in the music business, so I thought he might like it. But I think he gave it away."

"To?" Julie grabbed Christian's wrist.

"I don't know. Look, I'm tired and...anyway, this guy is on heavy meds and he's kind of loopy anyway, so you can't take what he says seriously. Julie! You're hurting my arm."

"Who'd he give it to?" She tightened her grip.

"Ow, ow, ow! He said he was going to give it to Clive..."

"Davis?"

"I think so."

"Clive Davis! Oh, fuck me! I just hung up on Clive Davis?"

Just then, the phone rang again.

Julie squealed, whipping her eyes from the phone back to Christian's face. "It's him." She dragged Christian to the table. "Answer it," she ordered, twisting his wrist.

"No way," Christian laughed. "You answer it. Ow! Careful, that's the arm I use to masturbate..."

"Ack!" Julie let go.

Christian picked up. "Hello?" He listened, with one finger pushed tightly across his lips. "Um, Julie Taylor? Uh-huh. I see. Oh, that girl who answered? No, she's not supposed to pick up, because she's...well, because she's a very angry foster child. I'll find Julie for you."

Christian motioned to Julie and clomped in a circle around the kitchen.

"May I tell her who's calling, please? Is that Clive with a 'v' or Clyde with a 'd'?"

Julie snatched the phone.

Aaron lay with one arm over his head, his fingers touching the rim of his ear. For hours he had lay there, trying to fall asleep, switching between sensual memories of his night with Christian and the guilt and anxiety of being a pariah in his own home. Rather than staying with his parents, he was haunting them—like a ghost they knew was there but refused to see. It was crazy-making. He'd gone home out of a sense of duty and love, but what love were they showing him?

Aaron's hand slid down to cup his genitals, a habit of self-comfort from his adolescence. Well, why not? Wasn't he now surrounded by the oddly juxtaposed fossils of his late boyhood? Model airplanes and rockets. A movie poster of Janet Leigh's terrified face in *Psycho*. A framed color portrait of Christ. Like his mother and father, the objects were familiar but disturbing. Like his parents, they belonged to the old Aaron.

Once he attained a fitful sleep, it was only a few minutes before he was roused by a warm tapping at his forehead. He opened his eyes to see a drop of blood hurtling down from the ceiling at his face. It landed and splattered off the bridge of his nose, right between his eyebrows, turning his vision a watery pink. He rubbed his eyes with his fists and blinked rapidly to clear them. On the ceiling, in a ragged loincloth and crown of briars, was a vision of himself as Christ on the cross. Blood streamed down from the nails in his hands and feet, soaking the bed...

"Why don't you just kill yourself?" asked the Christ. "Get it over with."

Aaron jerked awake. He sat up, hugging himself, and listened to the muffled sound of his parents' voices coming from the other end of the house.

Beached

Christian and Julie had turned the 6-by-8 patch of concrete off the back kitchen door of their bungalow into a makeshift beach plot. They scattered sand across it, placed a beach ball in one corner and an inflatable palm tree in the other, threw down tropical-colored towels, and brought out a yellow plastic sand shovel and pail filled with ice, limes, and a couple of Coronas.

That afternoon, the two stretched out in their bathing suits and donned big '70s sunglasses to bask in the brilliant November sun. After about 20 minutes, a single yellow leaf drifted down from a tree and landed on Julie's thigh. She sat up and stared at it.

"Hey, Christian."

"Yeah."

"Look at this."

He sat up, and they stared at the leaf together. A slight breeze blew across them, and the leaf trembled like a butterfly.

"That does it. It's official," said Julie. "Winter is here."

"Bundle up," said Christian.

In unrehearsed unison, each slid a pair of nylon shorts on, giggling as they settled back onto their towels.

"Ah," sighed Christian. "Much better."

"I agree," said Julie. "So," she went on. "They don't really like any of my songs for a video."

Christian shook his head. For the past week he had allowed himself to get swept into the excitement of Julie's career breakthroughs, listening patiently to her blow-by-blow accounts of this or that upcoming development and becoming her primary cheerleader through the inevitable moments of self-doubt. The role provided a needed distraction from his feelings about Aaron, which he preferred to downplay since there was nothing he could do about them.

"You're kidding me," he said. "What's that about?"

"Everything is so political in the music business." Julie squirted some sunscreen onto her chest. "I thought if I got signed, things would get easier."

"Hmm," said Christian. "Wish things would get easier for me."

"What's that supposed to mean? Oh, oh, wait," said Julie. "I almost forgot…there's this cute A&R guy from the record company, and he's being totally coy about which team he plays for."

Christian was bored already. "And?"

"I just thought I'd introduce the two of you. You can totally nail him and set the record straight—well, so to speak."

Christian shifted his spine. "Sorry, but I think I'll pass on this one."

"Get out! Why? He's totally cute. I'm serious." Julie rolled to her side and rose up on one elbow. "What's wrong with you anyway? You know, you haven't been yourself since… Wait—are you *still* not over Missionary Man?"

Christian turned to look at her. He pushed up his shades. "I don't know."

"You don't know?"

"Well, it's just weird, the way he disappeared like that. It's hard to just…"

"OK, then just stop moping like a schoolgirl and do something about it." She opened her eyes wide for emphasis. "Call him."

"How? Just dial 1-800-TORTUREDMORMON?"

"Probably—it sounds like there are enough of them to form a support group. But, if you want to know the truth, Christian, I think you should just get the hell over it. It's been almost two weeks now."

"Maybe I don't want to," he said irritably. "I mean, L.A. is a city where everyone dances with one eye on the door, like we're all waiting for that next something better to walk in. But would we even recognize it if it did? It might be nice to stop circling. It might be nice to stop equating sex with a handshake. It might be nice to have it *mean* something."

"Ooooh," cooed Julie, "listen to you…you are turning into a chick!"

"Shut up!" Christian jumped to his feet, grabbed the beer bucket, and headed for the door.

"Wait, Christian. Wait, seriously—you dropped something."

He turned. "What?"

"Your balls….they must have fallen off around here somewhere. Wait, let me check under here." She giggled and made a show of searching around.

Christian held up his hand. "All right. This is me not talking to you."

"But you'll still come to my show tonight, right?"

Judgment

Wind rustled the palm trees and multiple heads of hair along Sunset Boulevard as the usual crowd of hipsters and assorted tourists lined up along the sidewalk outside the Viper Room. Cool girls wearing thin jackets over spaghetti-strap mini-dresses clutched their elbows and waited to have their cigarettes lit by James Dean look-alikes while dark-clothed poseurs tried to look above it all. The house was packed, and the line just crawled along, at times immobile for minutes on end. Rows of cars cruised by, their self-conscious occupants deciding in advance that they weren't *something* enough—hip, young, glamorous, or important—to get in, and rolled on.

Inside, the crowd downed cocktails and grew restless for the band. Christian, Traci, and Andrew sat at the bar, cracking jokes and laughing giddily. They were nervous for Julie. There were agents there, and record companies, and they were there not to scope things out, not to search for new talent, but to hear the girl whose voice was— according to a certain source—"like cinnamon sticks in a cup of hot cocoa."

When the lights came up, the band kicked in full with a heavy beat, and Julie stalked onto the stage like a tiger in black velvet pants with stripes cut into the thighs. Her tight-fitting metallic crop-top revealed cut abs, amazing breasts, and arms that screamed stardom.

When you were just a child of eight
You were taught not to deviate
Only one way to heaven
But a half-million ways to fall...

Her voice, her look, and her moves were magnetic. The crowd pressed in close. Heads bobbed, hands went up.

"Damn, she looks fine," shouted Andrew. "Madonna, eat your heart out!"

He and Traci high-fived.

The whole group from Lila's was there. Carlos and five of his buddies pumped their fists and started moshing. Christian joined in with them.

It was a starkly cold evening in Pocatello. Several men in unstylish suits and overcoats trooped inside the boring brick and stucco structure of a large Mormon Church. They avoided looking at the black Dodge Durango in which Aaron Davis waited in angry silence with his father.

When the last man had gone in, Farron cracked open the frozen-shut door and put one steel-toed boot on the ground. He glanced back at his son, his eyes full of empathy. "I can't show you any favoritism."

"I know that," said Aaron. "I wouldn't want you to."

In the large, high-ceilinged church conference hall, 15 seated men clasped their hands and bowed their heads over a *U*-shaped arrangement of tables. At the base of the *U*, a serious and stressed-looking Farron Davis presided. He mumbled a quick opening prayer. On the other end of the room, at the open end of the *U*, Aaron sat in fearful defiance, his body language fully exposed in a lone folding chair.

"...Amen." Farron finished his prayer and lifted his head. The fluorescent overhead lights cast an austere glare off his bald dome. "As president of the Pocatello Stake, it is my unhappy duty and obligation to convene this church court on behalf of Elder Aaron Davis for the grave and grievous sin of homosexuality."

Aaron squinted his eyes against the blur of judgment surrounding him.

The acoustics of this large, almost featureless room were such that even the faintest sound produced a haunting echo. Various phlegmy throats rumbled in the silence that followed. Hands wrung. Atrophied butts shifted on chairs. And at the end of this symphony of acute discomfort, Farron leveled a weighted look at his son. "Do you feel ashamed of yourself?"

"It's kind of hard," he said, "to feel anything but ashamed."

"But are you remorseful?" prodded Farron. "No one can start on the long and painful path to true repentance without remorse." His mottled hands lifted from the table as he laced the tips of his fingers together and aimed them forward. "Are you deeply remorseful for this grave sin?"

Aaron eyed a patch of light on the floor. "I'm embarrassed, sure. I mean, to have you find out this way, to have

it all paraded out in public like this? Of course, it's humil-
iating. How do you expect me to feel?" He met his father's
eyes. "But am I sorry it happened? No."

Sagging eyelids widened. Murmurs—like smatters of
rain before a storm—carried across the room. Farron's
face flushed darkly. He drew in a breath. "This isn't easy
for me, Aaron. But in light of your abnormal and abom-
inable state, and your refusal to see that you've been
duped into some hogwash alternative lifestyle, I wish my
shame was enough for the both of us—not to mention the
shame you've brought to our church, our family, our
ancestors…"

"Wait a minute," said Aaron. He sat up tall in his chair.
"Our ancestors?" he added incredulously. "Dad, your
grandfather had at least a half-dozen wives, and the same
goes for every single person in this room. I'd say we were
the original definition of 'alternative lifestyle.' But now that
we've conveniently erased that episode from our theology,
that gives *our* church the right to define normal for everybody else? Don't you see what a contradiction that is?"

Farron stared impassively at his son. "Are you calling
us hypocrites?"

"Oh, no," whispered Aaron. "We've gone way beyond
hypocrisy, Dad. Now, we're just being mean."

Farron pointed his finger and his voice grew shrill. "I
will not be preached to, especially not by you, especially
not now." Recovering himself, he delivered his verdict in a
weighty monotone. "With the authority vested in me by
the Melkezedik priesthood and in the name of Jesus
Christ, I have no choice but to begin excommunication

proceedings against you, at which point you will be stripped of the priesthood, the garments, and your membership in this church."

Wordlessly, the men rose and filed from the room, unable to look at the cast-off young man who had once seemed to be such a promising member of their group.

Long Distance

Christian Markelli was obsessed.

It had been 48 hours since his last shower, and he still wore the same short navy sweatpants and baseball jersey he'd had on the day before. A lock of dirty hair straggled down his forehead. Wadded-up pieces of notebook paper, potato chip wrappers, and empty Starbucks cups littered the hot-pink area rug. He sat on the edge of the sofa, his knees spread apart as he hunkered down over the coffee table to tap at his laptop. On the floor near his chair was a CD-Rom for United States countrywide phone directories. His eyes narrowed and widened as he pored diligently over the screen, thumb-scrolling through numbers for the name Davis in the city of Pocatello, Idaho.

Julie passed through on her way to the kitchen. She was chomping on an apple and humming a tune she'd written whose lyrics continued to elude her. "Still at it, huh?"

"Yup," said Christian, his eyes glommed to the screen. "I'll say this much. There are a lot of Davises up there."

She leaned on the back of the sofa and peered over his shoulder. "Wow," she said. "You aren't exaggerating. Why don't you take a break? I know, let's go shoot some pool. We'll find ourselves some nice suckers…."

"Nah," he said, grinning. "It's tempting, but I can't. I've

got to finish this." He looked at her. "It's important to me."

"OK, good luck." She kissed the top of his head.

Seconds later, Christian dialed the phone and placed it to his ear. He waited while it rang, his left hand poised with a pink-glitter Hello Kitty pen over a scribbled-up page in his spiral notebook. "Aaron Davis. I'm trying to locate an Aaron Davis." He paused. "No? Thank you." He hung up the phone, checked his computer screen, then dialed the next number. As he waited for an answer, he distractedly doodled a Gothic-script number *9* in the margins of his notebook.

"No, I'm sorry," he said, adding a space-age *3* to his doodled numbers. "Not Errol. Aa-ron. Aaron Davis." He tapped the coffee table with his pen. "Two A's. No, no, he didn't win anything. No? Well, thanks anyway."

Christian ripped another page out of his notebook and hurled it to the floor with the others. He flopped back against one of furry blue throw pillows. Why was he even bothering? What if he had already called the house? That *was* a possibility, wasn't it? Why should anybody tell him anything? And what if he did get through? Would Aaron even want to talk to him? Hadn't he told Christian he would have to give up everything?

Christian closed his eyes, trying to quiet his doubt. It was impossible that Aaron didn't want to talk to him. He knew it in his heart. He sat up, leaned forward, and scrolled to the next page.

"Hello? Hello! Yes, hi. I'm looking for Aaron Davis."

"What?" squawked an old man's voice.

"I'm looking for Aaron Davis. Aa-ron Da-vis."

"What?" came the voice again. "You callin' from the dairy?"

"No! I'm calling from…" Christian started to hang up, but stopped himself.

"You want to talk to my wife? I'm supposed to have my hearing aid in—but I hate the flippin' thing."

"Yeah!" shouted Christian. "YEAH—LET ME TALK TO YOUR WIFE!"

Minutes seemed like hours as the man went to fetch her. Christian hoped she wasn't in the bathtub or anything like that. Too late—the image hit him: a stooped old man helping his pruny wife from the tub. Christian shook it off. He stared at a speck on the wall. His fingers drummed on the desktop.

"Hello?" said somebody's sharp old grandmother.

Christian's heart did somersaults. She sounded lucid.

"Hello. I'm trying to find someone named Aaron Davis."

"What?" said the woman. "The Davis boy?"

"Yes," said Christian. "Aaron. Blond hair, blue eyes…"

"'Bout 19?" she said. "Went to Californee on his mission?"

"Yes, yes. That sounds like him."

"He in trouble again?"

"No, no, he's not in any more trouble. What kind of trouble?"

"Well, partner," she quipped spryly, "if you don't know, I sure as heck ain't gonna tell you."

"No, that's OK, I don't mean to pry. I'm just a friend of his from California."

"Ha ha—that's all right. I'm just givin' you a hard time. Sounds like you're talkin' about Farron Davis's boy."

Christian scrolled frantically down his screen. "Farron Davis? Could you spell that?"

"F-a-r"—the woman cleared her throat vigorously—"-r-o-n."

Christian located the number. "Farron Davis on Stonecreek! Thank you so much."

"You're welcome. Now I got to get back to my *Hee Haw*. They got Buck Owens on, and he's singin' 'Rollin' In My Sweet Baby's Arms.' Hee, hee, hee…I just love that ol' tune."

"Uh, Buck Owens? They still run that?"

"Honey, out here in Idaho, they'll always be a-runnin' that."

"OK, well, you get back to it now. And thank you. Bye."

Christian hung up the phone and rubbed his hands together excitedly. He scrolled to highlight the name, telephone number, and address of Farron A. Davis, copied it into his notebook, and circled it. Suddenly, the lights flickered and the hairs on his neck stood on end. He reached for the wadded-up notebook paper he had just thrown to the floor. Unfolding it, he discovered seven randomly drawn digits, the digits that comprised Farron Davis's phone number.

It was three days before Thanksgiving, and in the yellow-walled dining room with its new holiday decor, Aaron and his mother were eating supper. Gladys finished up her last bite of green bean casserole and brought her red cloth napkin up to rest upon the busy harvest-print tablecloth. "What's wrong, Aaron? Is there something wrong with your dinner?"

Aaron dragged his fork through a mound of diced yams. "No, I'm just not hungry."

"I wish you would reconsider what we talked about the other day." Gladys folded her hands in front of her.

"I'm not going to any treatment center, Mom."

"But the Dyer center has a real nice facility, a real reputable program, and they can help you."

"Maybe…"

"Have you been praying on it?"

"I've done nothing but pray on it. I just don't think I need to be in a hospital."

"Oh, Aary, it isn't really a hospital—they do have an outpatient program. Did you look at the brochure? Let me go get it."

"Mom, I looked at the brochure…"

"Well, for crying out loud, you can't just spend the rest of your life moping around the house like this."

Just then the phone rang.

"I'll get it." Gladys walked quickly into the wood-paneled hallway between the dining and living room.

Aaron listened to her footsteps and contemplated the traditional travesty of their autumn foliage centerpiece. The arrangement of gold leaf–decorated plastic grapes and crabapples, silk maple leaves, and peach and white silk roses had been a gift from Aunt Nora in the early '90s, a relic from her failed silk flower arranging business. And every year the family carted it out and dusted it off for the week of Thanksgiving. Every year, the smell of it grew more musty and mothballish. Aaron dug at his food. That was probably his father calling to say he wouldn't make it for dinner again. His plate was still cooling at the head of the table, destined for another microwave warm-up.

"Hello?" said Gladys.

"Yes," came the voice at the other end. "Is Aaron Davis there?"

"I'm sorry, Brother Davis is down at the Stake Center—oh, I'm sorry, Aaron?" She threw a quick look over her shoulder, then scooted around the corner, stretching and untangling the phone cord behind her. Like a spy with a secret, she put her back to the wall, hunched over, and lowered her voice. "Um, may I ask why you're trying to reach Aaron?"

"I'm…a friend…"

"Mm-hmm…?"

"…from Los Angeles."

"A friend? Los Angeles, uh-huh. Well, are you one of the elders in Los Angeles?"

"Um…no, I'm not."

"No?" Gladys hugged herself.

"I'm sorry, can you tell him this is Christian calling?"

That predator! Her already blurry vision grew three times blurrier. She spoke through clenched teeth. "You know what? My son has no desire to speak with you…"

"But…" said Christian.

"…and I hope you will have the decency never to call here again."

Gladys brought the phone away from her ear and

calmly hung up as she passed through the hallway on her way back to the table. "Heavenly Father," she murmured in a soft whisper, "I thank you in the name of your son Jesus Christ…"

"Woo-hoo!" shouted Christian. "Hey, Julie, get in here."

Julie had fallen asleep in the middle of yoga pose. She ambled in drowsily, wearing blue sweatpants and a lavender leotard, with her sweatshirt tied around her waist.

Christian perched at the arm of the sofa. "I found him!"

"You talked to him?"

"No, but his mother just hung up on me."

Julie's mouth dropped open. "Bitch—"

"No, wait," prattled Christian. "If he really didn't want to talk to me, then she wouldn't have had a problem putting him on the phone so he could tell me himself, right? And next time, he'll probably pick up."

Julie put her hands on her hips and looked him up and down. "You're thinking, baby. It's new, but I like it."

Christian hugged her. "Well, damn, baby, who knew getting hung up on could make me feel so good?"

"That does it, then," said Julie. "We're finally going out. Because *you* have been a contrary Mary way too long."

Aaron had resumed digging through his casserole when his mother bustled up to the table with a false business-as-usual demeanor. "Everything OK, dear?"

"Yeah. Is Dad missing dinner again?"

"Hmm? Oh, no, that was nothing—just another

obnoxious telemarketer. But your Dad sure *is* late getting home from the Stake Center." She picked up his father's plate. "Well, there's no point in letting this get cold." She plodded into the kitchen to cover it with Saran Wrap. When she came back to clear the table, she paused to watch Aaron sadly digging through his food. "I'll take this one too," she said, jerking his plate out from in front of him. "If you're just going to play with it…" She rolled her eyes toward heaven as she hurried into the kitchen. "I don't know why I even bother anymore."

Aaron moped at the table, rolling an unappetizing piece of cold yam in his mouth. He wondered if Christian had ever tried to reach him. Suddenly he heard a loud crash from the kitchen and he got up and hurried to check on his mother. When he found her, he stopped and stared from the archway.

Gladys knelt on the kitchen tile gathering shards of a dropped plate. Her sluggish movements contrasted with the festively stenciled walls and cupboards, the wreaths, berries, and red apple cookie jar.

"Are you…" started Aaron. "Is everything OK?"

She continued her task without looking up. Her gray roots showed at the top of her head. "Yeah, I'm just a little dropsy. You go on."

Aaron watched her for a long moment.

"Mom."

"Uh-huh."

"Mom!"

She glanced at him with a brief flash of annoyance. "What, Aaron, what?"

"Nothing. I just wanted to see if you could bring your-self to look at me."

"I'm looking at you, Aaron." She grabbed the side of the counter to haul herself up from her knees. "What am I supposed to be seeing?"

"Nothing." Aaron walked away.

"His name was Christian," she called after him, "wasn't it?"

Aaron returned to the doorway. "What?"

He was trembling, and she saw it, and she hated him for it. "Was Christian the one?"

Before he could prevent it, Aaron's face radiated pure joy at the mention of the name.

Gladys's face screwed up. "What did he do to you?"

"He…" Aaron smiled, nodding happily. "He loved me."

"No! He didn't. Don't say that." Gladys put the bowl into the sink. "Do you know how ridiculous that sounds? How repulsive that is to God, to everyone? Two men?" She shook her head. "Men don't love, Aary. Women bring love to a relationship."

Aaron smiled wistfully. "He told me he loved me."

"He would've told you anything. He lied to you. He flattered you. Tools of the devil—that's what they do."

"You don't know that."

"I do."

"You don't know that, Mom."

"Yes, I do—you know why? Because when you didn't make it home that day I called your mission president."

"You checked up on me, huh?"

"I was worried sick about you. And do you know what he said? Your missionary companion told him that this

Christian person—you were nothing more than a bet he made."

"That's not true!" Aaron cried.

"Yes, it is true," corrected Gladys. "He won your soul for a lousy $50." She peeled off her gloves and threw them into the sink. "That's all you were worth to him. And you know what? He's probably already forgotten all about you and is moving on now to his next fornication."

"Mom, he wouldn't do that."

"Yes, he would. Don't you see? The whole thing meant nothing to him. He was using you. That's why you can never even think about him." She walked over to stand in front of her son. "Not ever, ever again."

Aaron's eyes filled with tears. *This doesn't have to mean anything.* Weren't those Christian's first words before they…?

"Aaron, listen to me. You have got to put this thing behind you," said Gladys. "This horrible mistake that everyone knows about. Everyone! You've seen how people look at us. You've seen how people just turn their carts around when we come down the aisle in the market. The way they look the other way at the bank. Why do you think your father never comes home? How can we ever hope to put what you've done behind us if…"

"What if it's not something I've done?" pleaded Aaron. "What if it's who I am?"

Gladys slapped him. "Don't say that! Don't you ever even think like that!"

Aaron covered his mouth and sobbed like a child. His

entire world was collapsing. Why should he even on living if he couldn't be who he was?

Gladys buried her face in her hands. When she finished crying, she lifted her head and said determinedly, "Aaron, you can be forgiven for what you did. With repentance and prayer and true, heartsick remorse, *maybe* Heavenly Father can forgive you for what you did. But who you *are*? He can never forgive something like that."

Aaron crumbled. He sank to his knees and curled into a fetal position with his shoulder against the wall. Gladys turned and walked back to the sink. Quietly and serenely, as if nothing had happened, she picked up the bowl that held the shards of plate and tossed them each one by one into the garbage. "You might want to pull yourself together," she said blandly—as if to no one but herself. "Your sister will be here in couple of hours, and you may want to think about what you're going to tell her."

The Perfect Man

"Two more?" asked the bartender.

"Why not?" answered Christian.

Their chosen nightspot teemed with its usual humidity, with the reckless sweat of the throng and the mad heat of the cruising and the cruised. Julie and Christian sat hemmed in at the bar doing 99-cent tequila shots. "Here," Christian shouted over the thudding base. "Let me."

He poured a sprinkle of salt into the space between Julie's thumb and forefinger. Then he did the same for himself. Having already downed a couple of shots and one beer each, the two watched each other as they licked away the salt, downed another shot, and dashed off to lose themselves among the others out on the dance floor.

Aaron paced back and forth across his bedroom. *You're worthless,* hidden voices told him. *What are you, scared?* He opened his closet and pulled down a large cardboard box with several stickers on it; among them was one that proclaimed FAMILIES ARE FOREVER. Aaron read it numbly and peeled apart the top flaps of the box. The box was filled with model rocket equipment, strips of balsa wood, and ancient tubes of glue. His hands moved decisively, tossing items aside in his search for the one thing he needed. He saw it. A balsa wood box. He pulled it out and slid the lid open.

Inside was a gleaming Exacto knife—its handle tinged with a few spots of rust but the carbon-colored blade still fresh.

In the kitchen, Gladys was still finishing up the dishes. She felt heartbroken about what had just happened between the two of them, especially the part about blaming Aaron for why his father was never home. That had been going on for a while and they both knew it. She was just taking out her anger on him, but why did he have to be so stubborn about all of this? If he would just try the reparative therapy program at the Dyer center.

She heard the back door close and looked up to find Aaron's sister entering in a thick wool coat with a heavy suitcase. Susan looked radiant. Her cheeks and lips were flushed with the cold. Her shoulder-length blond hair was powdered with light snowflakes.

"Mom, what's wrong?" She let go of her suitcase and fumbled—her chilled fingers clumsy—on the giant fuzzy buttons of her coat. "Where's Dad? Did something happen to Grandma?"

Gladys went to her. She flung her arms around her. "It's Aary...he's been sent home from his mission. I didn't know how to tell you... We didn't want to worry you during your exams."

"What?" said Susan. "How long has he been here?"

"A few weeks. It's been awful. I'm so sorry, honey. Thanksgiving's ruined."

"Forget about Thanksgiving, Mom. What happened?"

Gladys stared at her. Her voice dropped to a whisper. "Something terrible."

Inside the bathroom, Aaron never heard the front door shut. Susan's entrance and hysterical exchange with Gladys was muffled by the burble of running water filling the sink. He considered his eyes in the mirror. He despised himself. Nothing seemed possible anymore. Not Christian. Not his mother. Not his father. Not love. Steam filled the bathroom, like a soothing cloud of balm, fogging the mirror in front of him. The water rose. The Exacto knife rested almost weightlessly in his hand. He placed it on the edge of the white porcelain sink, where it glistened in the sterile light.

Aaron removed his clothes. He hung them carefully over the hook on the back of the bathroom door. He buried his hands under the water in the sink, tightening and relaxing his fists like a junkie trying to bring forth a vein. Swiping his hand across the mirror, he took another look at himself through the residue of moisture. But his face was quickly obscured by the steam.

As it should be.

He picked up the knife.

Christian and Julie held center court to a throbbing electronic medley. They put their hearts and guts into it, grooving and working it like the old days—and the old days were only months ago. Julie felt like she'd gotten her best friend back, and she never wanted to lose him again.

She peeled off Christian's shirt to the appreciative stare of a tattoo-covered hunk in camouflage pants. Christian tossed his head. Sweat spattered off him and baptized the crowd.

Blood spattered Aaron's feet, but he was far, far away. The overflowing sink was like a roar in his ears. His numb arms dropped limply, and he slid naked to the floor. His head lolled back, thudding softy against the linoleum. Pink water trickled over the edge of the sink and onto his chalk-white forehead.

Christian threw out his arms and spun in a circle. The hunk in camo pants grooved his way across the floor, muscles shifting like hurricane clouds. As Christian ended his spin, the hunk leaned in, reached out his tattooed arms, and kissed Christian on the lips. "I'm tweaking," he mouthed.

Christian pulled back. The music thumped like a frantic heartbeat. He gazed coolly at the tweaker; his eyes said "thanks, but no thanks." He patted the guy's meaty chest. He was miles away from all this. The tattooed man had beautiful green eyes that seemed to look at Christian with sympathy. They shared a surreal moment that was halfway between seduction and understanding. Showing off, the man drew his fingers up the sweaty bumps of his abs, but in his sexy smirk. Christian saw nothing but a perfect man with a secretly sad smile. He shrugged, shaking his head. The man whirled away, his back shimmering like a fish, until he disappeared, sucked back into the thrashing masses.

Christian watched him go. He unlooped his shirt from his belt, waved to Julie, and blew out of the club.

Julie threw out her hands. "What's wrong with you?"

Susan knocked on the bathroom door. "Hey, Aary. Hey, bro. How ya doing?"

She put her lips to the corner. "Hey, look, I just talked to Mom. Look, I know things are kind of rough right now. But you know that, as far as I'm concerned, nothing has changed between us. You know that, right? Aary? You get that, right?"

She shifted awkwardly. Her right foot squished. She looked down, puzzled at the dark stain that seeped into the carpet.

Don't Take It Personally

A cold wind buffeted the family SUV as it crunched over the snowy gravel in the Davis household's driveway. Farron climbed out in his dated black suit. Gladys emerged in a somber charcoal sweater set. The two headed for the house, trudging across the icy earth in intentionally separate trajectories.

Inside, Gladys stared dully at the Polaroids of the family stuck with alphabet magnets all over the refrigerator door. What had happened to all this? How could they ever recover?

"I'll heat up that casserole," she called out reflexively, still staring at the photos, "with the cream of mushroom soup."

When there was no answer from Farron, she turned to see him gathering up his keys and satchel. There were lines in his face she had never noticed before—and the others had grown deep as cuts.

"Where are you going?"

He picked up his hat. "Got some stuff to do down at the church."

"Now? But we just came back..." She choked on her words. "Your son...we just came back from..."

Farron could not look at her. "It's as good a time as any."

The sound of the door closing behind him echoed like the sound of a slap.

Gladys was left alone with herself. She grabbed the kitchen counter with one hand and hallucinated that the walls were speeding away from her, leaving her more and more alone in a larger and larger space. Her pinched half-smile trembled. Who was she saving it for? Her hand fluttered up to her chest, and she fainted.

Sprawled on her side, her skirt hiked up around her thick hips, Gladys drifted in and out of blackness. When the phone rang she sat up with a jerk. It rang again. She climbed slowly to her feet. For some odd reason, she had the presence of mind to remove a clip-on earring on the way down the hall.

She cleared her throat. "Hello?"

"Mrs. Davis. I know that you don't want me to speak to your son…"

Gladys gripped the receiver in a stranglehold. Her half-smile was still frozen in place, but her eyes saw red as she fought for her breath. "My son?" she said spiteful-ly. "My son? Listen to me, you son of a bitch. Thanks to you, my son took a razor to his wrists." She removed the receiver from her ear—she didn't want to hear him. And her clenched fist rotated the mouthpiece to her lips. "I have lost my son, thanks to you, and I hope you burn, I hope you burn forever, I hope…" Gladys's arm fell to her side, and her hand jerked open. The receiver bounced on the end of its coil and banged noisily into the wall.

Julie dragged herself through the front door in one of Christian's white button-down shirts, which hung all the way to the knees of her jeans. She was beat after another long morning at the recording studio. "Damn," she said, thinking she was alone. "I need a Diet Coke or something." She blew out a tired sigh, kicked off her flip-flops, and dropped her purse on the sofa on her way to the kitchen. Halfway there, she spotted Christian sitting frozen at the table, still holding the phone in his hand.

"Hey, what are you…? Are you OK?"

Her presence startled him out of his shock. He broke into guttural gasps.

"Oh, my God, Christian—what happened?"

She went to him. He hurled his enormous arms around her waist and stared up at her. "Aaron's dead."

"What?"

He buried his face in her shirt.

The activity at Lila's had dwindled down to its last few customers, who lingered over coffee as if they would never leave. Christian bussed tables, a morose shadow amid linen tablecloths. Lila watched him. From behind the bar, she picked up a couple of shot glasses and a bottle.

Catching sight of his boss on the way over, Christian stepped it into high gear.

She sauntered up behind him. "Christian."

"I'm sorry," he blurted out. "I'm sorry, it's just that…"

"Sit," she said, pouring out the brandy.

Resigned, Christian slid into the booth.

Lila put the bottle down. She slid in across from him. She stared into his heartsick eyes and picked up her glass. "Drink."

They touched glasses. Christian took a small sip.

"Toss it," ordered Lila. "That way it's medicinal."

They both threw the brandy back. Christian exhaled with the heat of it. Lila refilled their glasses. "One more"—she smiled—"doctor's orders." They threw back the second round. "Good," she said. "It's vital for a man to have a couple of slugs in him when discussing heartache. I think Hemingway told me that."

Christian put on his bravest face. "You knew Ernest Hemingway?"

"Margaux, actually." She smirked wryly at her own joke, then placed a cool hand over his. "You know, Christian? Beauties don't always escape tragedy."

His facade wouldn't hold. "Oh, God. This...this is hell. I've done something horrible. I'm guilty, and I'll burn for it."

"Funny thing about guilt," said Lila. "There's nothing so bad that you can't add a little guilt to it and make it worse. But there's nothing so good that you can't add a little guilt to it and make it better."

Christian looked at her. "But I..."

"Hush, child. You're not going to burn."

"No?"

"No. Guilt distracts us from a greater truth—that we have an inherent ability to heal. We seem intent on living through even the worst heartbreak."

"How?" asked Christian.

"Practice." She patted his hand gently and poured another drink. "And one more just for practice." She raised her glass. "Remember, that which doesn't kill us"—she paused dramatically—"sometimes leaves us maimed for life." She reached out for Christian's cheek and caressed it.

"But the only way to find out is to face it head-on."

Lila stood and wove her way back to the office, leaving Christian alone in the dim yellow light. But how could he face what wasn't there? He moved out of the booth, picking up their shot glasses. But on his way to the bus cart, he paused. He reached into his pocket and pulled out Aaron's watch.

In the soft glow of a lonely strand of Christmas lights, Christian sprawled on the sofa in what Julie called his "raggedy-ass sweat bottoms," scratching a journal entry into his PDA.

The key turned in the lock at the front door. It was Julie coming home after another long day.

Christian gaped at her, throwing a hand to his chest like a scandalized school marm. "After 3?" he scolded. "You slut."

"I wish," said Julie. She rolled her eyes. "We were in the studio. What about you?"

Christian clicked off his journal. "Couldn't sleep."

Julie flopped down next to him. "So, what? You sit here in the dark? Hey, I know—let's just say fuck the no-carb thing and go to Dupar's and eat pancakes till we choke, huh? What do you say?"

"Nah." Christian shook his head. "I think I'll just go back to bed." He hefted himself up and hobbled stiffly to his bedroom, closing the door.

"Good thing I don't take rejection personally," she called after him, knowing he probably couldn't hear her. She pulled her bag from her shoulder and fished out her notebook, leafing through pages of so-so lyrics and grow-ing more and more depressed. Crossing her arms over her notebook and sighing, she honed in on Christian's PDA on the coffee table. She looked to Christian's bedroom, hesitated, then grabbed it. She clicked it on and slid out the stylus, pulling up her roommate's last entry.

It's 3 a.m., and once again I can't sleep. It's like I'm waiting for time to fix some part of me that keeps on breaking. I've already thrown out the newspaper. And I've washed the leftover dishes. Nothing to do but sit here and think…

Julie read the words again. *Now, this is raw. This is what I need to tap into.* She placed the PDA back down on the table and—with its pale-blue light blanketing her face—copied the entry word for word into her notebook.

You Have That Look

Raindrops sparkled on the windowpane. Christian was reading the paper to Keith. "The attackers fled after being fired…on…" He looked up. Keith had dozed off.

Slowly and quietly, Christian set aside the paper. He scrutinized the vase of fading daisies he'd brought the last time he visited. *Time for some fresh ones.* He heaved himself out of the chair, picked up the vase, and headed for the kitchen.

"Just where do you think you're going with my goddamn flowers?"

Christian turned defensively. "But they're…"

"We don't throw anything out that's not completely dead. Deal?"

They stared at each other.

"Deal," Christian said, putting the vase back.

"And another thing," said Keith. "You've got to quit coming over here and moping around. You're fucking depressing me."

Christian's eyebrows shot up. "I'm depressing *you*?" He took a seat next to Keith.

"That's what I'm saying." Keith turned up his palm. "And if we've reached the point that you're dragging on my day, we've got a problem." He reached out to put a hand over Christian's. "Seriously," he said, "you've got to do something. You have to make a move. Find a way to get past this."

Christian tried to smirk but could not pull it off. "What, are you being the oracle guy again?"

"No," said Keith. "I'm just being a friend."

The barrettes in Gladys's hair quaked with the motion of her head as she rapidly scrubbed the stove element with a five-year-old dish brush. A high-pitched righteous hymnal blared on the stereo: *When other helpers fail and comfort flee...*

The front doorbell rang. *Ding-dong.*

Gladys stripped off her red rubber kitchen gloves as she walked to the stereo and turned down the volume. She bent back a few times, stretching out her spine like her physical therapist had taught her. She'd been seeing one for three weeks now, ever since her sciatica started acting up. The bell sounded again. She walked briskly to the door—*Whatever happened to manners?*—pulling her knitted blue sweater tight across her stomach in anticipation of the bitter icy wind. It had been like that since Thanksgiving, ever since...

Gladys opened the door. "Hello, may I help you?"

In front of her was a tall, gorgeous young man in a black snow hat, black jeans, a black turtleneck, and a long black leather dress jacket. A charcoal-gray vinyl satchel hung at his hip. His olive skin was flawless in the cold afternoon light. His black eyes burned with sorrow. Who was he? A local elder?

He stood respectfully, with his head slightly lowered and his hands folded in front of him. "Are you Aaron Davis's mother?"

She shrugged and nodded guardedly. "I'm Sister Davis, yes."

"I knew your son," he said. "In Los Angeles."

"Oh, you must be one of the elders from there." She eyed his satchel. "You…you have that look."

"No," he said gently. "My name is Christian." He uncrossed his hands. "He lost his watch." Christian began to cry as he revealed the tarnished silver timepiece. "I wanted to let you know how sorry I am. It kills me to think that I"—he placed the watch in Gladys's palm and with his hands closed her small fingers around it—"that I could've caused him any pain."

He fled down the walk.

Gladys watched him get into his rental car. *He left the motor running,* she noticed dully. She went back inside the house, in shock, listening to the car make a three-point turn in the gravel driveway and clutching the watch in physical pain. All the mental tirades, all the fantasized recriminations she had heaped upon this predator…where were they? *What kind of person?* she wondered. *What kind of person would travel so far just to…* She popped open the watch and stared at the internal engraving:

THE GREATEST

OF THESE IS

CHARITY

1 COR 1345

Gladys staggered slightly as waves of remorse washed over her.

He doesn't know…

She ran to the door. His car was just pulling onto the road. She sprinted across the porch and into the driveway, waving her arms. "Wait! Wait!"

But it was too late.

She craned her neck for a last look at him.

As she walked back to the house, she checked the mailbox and found a letter from Susan.

Dear Mom,

You have no idea how many times I've started this letter in my head. Since all this happened it's been hard, to say the least, to concentrate on my studies. None of it seems that important, if you know what I mean. I keep blaming myself and wondering how I failed my big brother. I wonder if all this could've been avoided if I'd only paid attention to things that were always staring me in the face. Or if only I'd done this or that or at least something…

So I'm sure you're suffering more than anyone over what happened, blaming yourself, thinking you've failed as a mother, but you have to stop that, all right? Nobody made Aaron gay, OK? And you were a great mother and still are.

Anyway, you've heard me say all this before—I mean, it's not like we haven't talked about it or anything, right?! But I did some research last night on the Internet and I have some maybe surprising and maybe not so surprising news for you. You're not the only parent of a gay son in Pocatello. You're not the only Mormon parent of a gay son either. (I know you don't like the word "gay" and probably hate me calling him that, especially considering where he is now—but I believe it is the truth.)

I've enclosed a couple of things I printed out last night off various Web sites. One is the PFLAG (Parents and Friends of Lesbians and Gays) home page. I wrote the phone number of the Pocatello chapter at the top of the printout. The other is this group of Mormon parents of gay children... Just hold off on judging right now and take a look at what they have to say. I think, if nothing else, it might help you feel less isolated....

Christian parallel-parked his RAV4 about a half-block away from his apartment. He wrapped his coat around him and dashed along the black, glimmering sidewalk. The rain pelted down. Christian misstepped into someone's lawn and twisted his ankle in a sprinkler well. Brown water filled his shoe.

His desperate act, returning the watch, had done nothing but make his pain more real. Aaron's mother's eyes had been so cold. Now, he felt her blame and hatred following him everywhere. The memory pierced his chest and twisted in his heart like a blade.

He wiped off his shoes outside the door and checked the mail. There was a large stack of magazines and catalogs. He grabbed it all. A strong, wet breeze kicked in just as he was bending his head to sort through it, and an envelope—some kind of bill—slipped off the top and fluttered over the edge of the steps into the mud. He tramped down and around to retrieve it—the power bill. As he shook the soggy envelope, he glanced at the jagged edge of the hose holder. He remembered the cut, and the gentleness of

Aaron's hand dabbing at him with the washcloth. Their moment on the bed. Their night in the hotel.

Was it really only just a few months ago?

Christian clutched the mail to his chest and weeped.

By the time he pulled himself together enough to get aside, he's thoroughly soaked.

Through the darkness, he spied Julie on the sofa in front of the television, her legs stretched out across the coffee table, with a blanket over her lap. There were crumbs on the blanket, as if she'd finished a snack hours ago and hadn't bothered to clean up. Her face was expressionless as the flickering light from the screen danced over it.

"Jeez," Christian mumbled. "This is almost too spooky. Maybe we should just get married."

She looked up at him. "What?"

"Never mind—just a joke."

"Well, anyway, hey," she said.

"Hey," said Christian.

"Oops, sorry." She brushed the crumbs to the floor. "What'd you do, take a shower in your clothes?"

"Nuh-uh. I couldn't find parking. I had to walk."

"That's no fun."

Christian pulled off his socks, wrung one out over a houseplant, and sighed. "Could be worse"—he pulled off his shirt—"could be raining." He sidled up next to her. "Oh, yeah—it is raining."

Julie stared at the screen. "Only in L.A.," she said, "does rain lead the 11 o'clock news as 'Operation Storm Watch.'" Her eyes fell to the disintegrating wet pile of magazines and catalogs in his lap. "Is that the mail?"

He yawned at her. "Yup."

"Any bills of mine in that pile? Oh, wait, what's this?" She fingered the corner of a fat, brown padded envelope.

Christian lifted the top half of the mail so she could slip it out.

"Oh, my God," she said, opening the envelope. "It's a copy of my video."

"What?" Christian sat up to show his interest. "Get outta here, it's about damn time. I've been waiting to see this." He nudged her ribs.

Julie stared at it, swallowed, and looked wracked with fear.

"Come on, girl—it's been so top secret. Plug it in. Let's go."

But she couldn't do it. Her hands were trembling.

"Aw, honey, there's nothing to be nervous about. Here…let me." He took the tape from her and crossed the room to the television.

She reached out. "No."

"Uh-uh, honey, this is no time for nerves. It's show-time." He paused to read the white encased videocassette. "'Love Letter. Artist: Julie Taylor'—I love it!—'Unedited commercial sample for reviewing purposes only.' Well, that's just what we're about to do, isn't it?" He opened the case, popped out the cassette, and…

Julie sprang off the couch. "No, I'll do it."

Christian handed it to her. "Well, OK. Let me just take my seat then. He crossed back to the other side of the room and arranged himself with one arm stretched out across the back rim of the sofa. "OK," he said, rubbing his hands together. "Let 'er rip."

Julie slowly plugged in the tape. She faced Christian,

holding the remote like a shield in front of her face.

"Girlfriend, come on," he said. "I'm sure I'll love it."

"OK," she said, "I'll play it, but just…I just don't want you to snap to some judgment."

"What?" he asked. "Is this some kind of, like, nasty-ass Christina Aguilera skankorama kind of video?" He leaned forward and laughed uncomfortably. "Or what…?"

"No…it's just…" She hit play, took a distant seat in a chair next to the TV, then stared at the screen.

Christian glanced at his friend.

This is a big moment for her. So why does she look like she's waiting her turn at the guillotine?

But he didn't have time to consider it further. A light came up on the screen, an orchestral thrum filled the room, and Julie appeared, dressed in a gossamer white gown. She drifted along the frame in a barren winter landscape.

"No flash cuts?" joked Christian. "No hootchie girls?"

The camera did a slow pull in on Julie pouring her heart out:

Tuesday, 3 A.M.
Once again I'm wide awake.
I'm waiting for time to mend this part of me
That keeps on breaking.

Christian's face darkened as he stared at the screen. "What the fuck?"

Newspapers I threw away.
Washed the dishes in the sink.

3 A.M. on Tuesdays
I have too much time to think.

"That's from my journal. What the *fuck* is stuff from my journal doing in here?"

"Hey," she ventured. "You were the one always asking me to write a song about you."

"What? And you think that meant…"

"And I was gonna tell you, or ask you, or whatever, I just…"

Christian got up and stood over her with his finger in her face. "But you knew I'd tell you to go fuck yourself, so you what"—he walked in a circle—"you steal my most private personal hell that I've been trying to get past, and you…you turn around and throw it back in my face? Is that it?"

Julie got up. "OK, OK—but let's just turn down the drama queen knob a notch…"

"I'll show you a drama queen knob!" Christian hurled a sofa pillow against the wall. "There, that's down a notch."

"If you'd listen to the song!" shouted Julie. "It's not all about you, you know, it hasn't been easy for me either." She sank back down onto the sofa and buried her face in her hands. When she looked up, her face was drenched in tears. "You don't think I wonder if I hadn't egged you on, hadn't pushed the whole damn game, he might not have… You ever think I might feel really shitty about that?"

Christian folded his arms. "Am I supposed to comfort you?"

"No, but don't fucking shut me out. I just thought something good could come out of this."

"Yeah, for you maybe."

"Jesus, Christian. I can't do this. I can't watch my best friend bury himself in misery like he's fucking Kurt Cobain—"

"Then don't try to be fucking Courtney Love and capitalize off it."

The phone rang. They froze, wondering, *How could someone call in the middle of this?* Julie grabbed it. "Hello. What? This is Julie. Yeah. OK." She glanced at Christian, who was tapping his foot and staring at the wall. "That's great. Yeah. No, I'm just in the middle of something. Thanks. I will. Bye." She shut off the phone and rested her head resignedly against the sofa.

"What?" asked Christian.

"That was New York. They want me for some video show or something."

"That's great—my own personal anguish as a mass-marketed product for teenage mall rats, anguish stolen from me by my best friend. You didn't even trust me enough to ask?"

"You know, anybody else might just try to be a little happy for me."

"Oh, I'm sorry. Congratulations."

"Jesus, Chris." She reached for his arm. "I didn't want to tell you like this… But the record label…they want me to move to New York for a few months. Because all the hot producers…they work in the clubs there."

Christian turned to her. "Have a nice trip."

Reparations

All the softer trappings of the living room were gone now, replaced by half-packed boxes littering the floor.

Christian slept in the dim shadows of his room. He moaned and flipped over, wincing and twitching as if in pain. In his dream he was seated in the middle of a stark-white room, strapped naked to an execution chair. Behind a window panel on the far left wall, two gleeful doctors in white shirts and ties took turns pressing buttons on a little black box the size of a Bible. Christian's eyes traced a set of four gray wires running from this wall. They trailed along the white tile floor, ran up his leg, and ended in a four-pronged suction sponge electrode that was strapped tightly around his crotch. He could feel a wet patch against his back. *Must be the ground electrode,* he mused calmly.

On the wall in front of him, the projected life-size image of a blond naked man flashed.

Was that Aaron?

ZZZZttt!

An electric pulse fried his genitals. He jerked in the chair, flexing his neck and biting down on a white washcloth they'd stuffed into his mouth. He strained at his wrist and arm restraints. Slowly, the charge dissipated.

The slide flashed off, then on to another image of Aaron. Christian braced himself for the second shock. He screamed. Suddenly he was seeing Aaron strapped into the chair. Christian was now a projected image on the wall. He felt his body changing from pinup pose to pinup pose. He was forced to watch as Aaron's eyes bulged red and his neck tensed up then slackened with each jolt. *ZZZZttt!* The doctors punched their buttons gleefully. *ZZZZttt! ZZZZttt!* Faster and faster. Christian screamed.

"Christian! Wake up!"

It was Julie, shaking him.

"Wake up, wake up…it's just a bad dream."

Christian's eyes fluttered open but remained blank with fear. He was still trapped in the dream.

She swiped a damp lock of hair from his forehead. "It's OK," she murmured, hugging and rocking him. "I'm here now."

Scooting along on his hands and knees, a blank-faced young man in institutional pajamas scrubbed the grout between weathered, oatmeal-colored floor tiles. Ever since his parents signed him in at the Dyer Mental Health Facility (whose south wing was devoted to "reparative therapy"), Aaron Davis had gone a bit mad. Every night at 3 A.M., he'd sleepwalk into the hallway to obsessively scour the grout. The orderlies had long since tired of waking him up. The kid would go ballistic whenever they did, and there was a tacit agreement on the night shift that restraining him just wasn't worth the headache.

Thunder rolled, a rarity in wintertime. Rain turned to

sleet against glass doors beyond locked wire mesh. Aaron muttered to himself in his sleep as he sawed back and forth with a pastel-blue toothbrush: "Must be worthy…must be worthy…must be…" Suddenly an awesome clap of thunder rocked the hallway as an almost simultaneous flash illuminated his face. He woke abruptly. "Huh?"

It was the only time he'd been jolted awake by something that hadn't caused him to get violent.

Perhaps it was because of the sound beyond the rain, an orchestral sound that floated down the hall, familiar but out of place.

Something musical, yes.

The voice of an angel.

Aaron pushed himself to his feet. He walked to the recreation room, where bored night-shift orderlies sat playing gin and drinking coffee. None of them noticed him there in the doorway. There was a TV mounted high in one corner, tucked safely inside a wire cage.

There she is, thought Aaron. *I knew it was her voice.*

Raspy—almost like a man's, but finer.

Julie wandered across the screen in a white gossamer gown.

Tuesday, 3 A.M.
Once again I'm wide awake.
I'm waiting for time to mend this part of me
That keeps on breaking.

Newspapers I've thrown away.
Washed the dishes in the sink.

3 A.M. on Tuesdays
I have too much time to think.

As she sang, a caption scrolled across the lower part of the screen: *Julie claims this song isn't about a boyfriend, but about her roommate's heartbreak…*
Aarons stared, trembling, at the screen. So it was real. It had meant something after all.

Nothing here can bring you back.
He has nothing left to show,
But a pocket watch
and the memory of a kiss out in the snow.
I hear him call up to heaven
I watch him crawl down to hell
He's not getting over you
And I know he never will.

"He's not getting over me," shouted Aaron.
"What?" A 300-pound thug looked up from his cards. "What'd you say, Toothbrush?"
"He's not getting over me!" repeated Aaron. "He's not getting over me! He's not getting over me!" He sprinted back down the hallway to his room.

Los Angeles

In the city of Hollywood in an empty Spanish bungalow courtyard surrounded by moonlit palms and eucalyptus trees, a tired but hopeful young man hesitated at the blue-painted door of apartment 3B. This was the first time he had been here in a very long time and, despite his certainty that there was something real between him and Christian, he was having a confidence crisis. Aaron ran his fingers through his travel-flattened hair, sniffed his thin acrylic sweater, and was resisting the urge to run back to his cab when he noticed the shadow of a small potted cactus plant jutting large across the stucco. *It has to mean something*, he decided, *for something as small as a cactus to become so important.* He knocked. The door swung inward. Aaron squinted at the shadowy figure standing—no, *posing*—in the shadows: shirtless, tanned, a study in sculpted perfection. The figure leaned sleepily in the doorway.

"Huh?"

Aaron stood at the top of the steps, looking pale and gaunt as an apparition.

The figure did not recognize him. "Can I help you with something?"

"Um. I was looking for Christian."

"Um, yeah. Christian's not here, he…"

"Oh, sorry. Never mind." Aaron turned and paced quickly away.

"Wait," called the man. "Did you want me to give him a message or something?"

But Aaron was already gone, stumbling dejectedly down the steps to the sidewalk.

Christian absentmindedly sampled a few fries from a plate left on the order counter. He was the same man, in the same place, but there was a subtle difference in his face—an almost wizened quality. It detracted from the prettiness but deepened his beauty. "Hey, Carlos, could I get some more fries here, please?"

Lila entered, looking lovely in a brown velvet suit.

"Mr. Markelli, I though I might introduce you to a special celebrity guest we have here with us this evening…"

"This should be good," said Christian.

He expected her to usher him out into the restaurant, but instead she held the door aside.

"May I present the lovely and talented Miss Julie Taylor!"

Julie stepped in, looking radiant.

"We've met," said Christian.

"Then perhaps," said Lila, smiling. "I should leave you two alone." She executed a seamless turn and discreetly disappeared.

"Hi," said Julie.

"Hi."

"I've just got a layover before I fly to Seattle to start the tour. Just the opening act—but, hey."

"You'll be great," said Christian. "Break a leg."

"I just…didn't want to leave things the way we did."

Christian waved his hand, brushing it off.

"No," said Julie. "Really. Are you OK?"

"I still have moments when I feel like I'm about to fall apart. I definitely don't have it together yet. But at least I feel like all the pieces are there, you know?"

"I think I know what that feels like."

"Yeah?" He sighed. "That's good, because I'm not sure what I mean."

Julie approached him, reaching into her bag. "I brought you something." She held out a small wrapped package.

Christian took it gingerly. He carefully pulled at the wrapping paper.

"Ugh," said Julie. "Not like that. It's not a Fabergé egg or anything. Who do you think I am, Madonna?" She snatched at the paper.

He shoved her away, laughing. "All right, I'm tearing it. See? This is me, tearing."

Their eyes meet for a moment. "Just like old times," she said punching his shoulder.

Christian finished ripping the paper off. He examined the gift. "Oh, it's a…what is it?"

"It's a journal. But this one's got a lock on it, so you can keep out nosy roommates…or whoever."

Christian pointed to the cover. "Hello Kitty?"

"And it's got secret sparkle pages," said Julie. "For special days." She suddenly turned somber. "I'm so sorry, Christian. Promise me you don't hate me."

"Oh, honey." He held his arms out. "Promise me I won't hear you on the radio and say, 'Hey, I used to know that girl.'"

"Shut up. We're family. That's not gonna change."

"But still," said Christian. Holding out his finger, he went into E.T. mode: "Ooouuuuch." He touched his chest.

"I'll be right here," said Julie. "Oh, shit, I'm going to miss my flight. But you be well. And use those sparkly pages. Have some special days." Julie pulled herself away. She turned at the swinging doors, blowing Christian a kiss. "Hot stuff," she said wistfully. "Comin' through."

"Hot stuff," he said with her. "Comin' through."

She slipped out through the doors.

Christian was left in the constant clatter of the kitchen. He watched the doors swing close on a part of his life. He looked at the journal and opened it. The first page shone back at him, a happy yellow. He smiled sadly, plucked a pen from his apron, and scrawled something.

The number 2 bus grumbled off in a cloud of black exhaust. Aaron was left on the sidewalk in front of the Chevron across from Virgin Records Megastore. The wrinkled and worn business card had a phone number and a handwritten note on the back. "Please come see me!" He flipped it over to double-check the address: just a few blocks south.

He adjusted his satchel and started down the sidewalk. A woman with fuchsia hair in short bangs, black lipstick, and snake tattoos running up and down her arms strolled by, holding hands with her boyfriend, who was dressed as a '50s gas station attendant. He even had one of those hand-stitched name-tags. It said *Roger*. "Hey there," she said as they went past one another. "Hey there," said Aaron. "Hey, Roger."

"What's up?" said Roger.

"Do you know where Lila's restaurant is?"

"Lila's? Um, yeah—it's down about a block and a half more."

"Thank you."

"No problem. See ya."

Aaron was exhilarated to be free of his companions and rigid schedule. Los Angeles felt more vivid to him. The chaos busier, the traffic louder, and the foul smell thick as a taste in his mouth. But rather than disappointing Aaron, or annoying him, or disgusting him, it all just felt more alive. The city wasn't any different. Only he had changed. At the temple he'd made promises to God. On a Greyhound to Los Angeles he'd made promises too—to himself *and* to God. Nothing, not anger, not love, not temptation would be shut out anymore.

As his new self, the real Aaron, everything—good and bad—was his to embrace.

Traci morosely entered the kitchen. "Order up," she droned, dinging the little bell.

Andrew sliced lemons at the counter. "Sorry, kid. I heard you didn't get the part."

"Motherfucker producer," said Traci. "Is that redundant?"

"Yes," said Andrew. "I believe it is. Hate to admit it, but I'll miss you when you go back to New York."

"Who said anything about leaving?"

"Let's see, I thought you did. Just last week you said, 'If I don't get this part, then…'"

"Um, look, Andrew. If you tell anyone I said this, I'll rip your lips off. I was miserable in New York."

"But you're miserable here too."

"Yeah, but at least in L.A. you can be miserable with a tan."

"I heard that."

Aaron stood feeling totally out of place amid the hip clientele who loitered about the lobby waiting for their tables. Then he spotted Lila. She looked beautiful and was only a short distance away—in the middle of relaying an apparently hilarious anecdote to a table full of rapt, paunchy men in expensive clothing.

As the men laughed and rocked tearfully over their plates, Lila looked up, noticed Aaron, and suddenly excused herself. She moved smoothly across the room.

He took some tentative steps forward.

"My dear boy," she said warmly.

Aaron held up her business card. "I was hoping this was still good."

She hugged him. "Of course it's still good."

As they pulled away from each other, he added, "I…didn't have any other place to go."

Disarmed, Lila smiled. "Welcome." She looped her arm under his and grasped his hand reassuringly. "Come on," she said. "Sit with me." She ushered him over to the bar. "Andrew, give my young friend here whatever he likes." She nodded at Aaron. "Well, what'll it be?"

"Uh, just a Coke, thank you." He smiled sheepishly.

"Nothing stronger?" prodded Lila. "You look like you could use it. If you don't mind me saying, you look like, well… hell. Why?"

Aaron eyed a water stain on the bar. "I didn't come to unload on you."

"Why not?" said Lila. "You gave me the opportunity once. Let me return the favor."

Aaron took comfort in Lila's soothing hand on his. "All right. After we met," he began, "I was sent home and excommunicated from my church…for being gay."

"Your church doesn't like alcohol or gay people? Hmm… Then I'm definitely not joining. I can't imagine heaven without both." She ducked her head and winced at her own corny humor. "Sorry, go on."

Aaron's Coke arrived. He sniffed it once, then took a massive swig. "It led me to a"—he wiped his lips—"brief but disastrous affair with a sharp object."

Lila watched him take another drink. His sleeve slid up enough to reveal rows of raised purplish scars.

Aaron set down his glass. "After the hospital stitched me up, my parents put me in this place—this facility where they were supposed to change me, fix me." He sighed and shook his head. "Then one night I was out in the hallway. I was…cleaning this floor with a toothbrush. That's when I heard it. This voice. It was like an angel. But it was just the TV. We weren't even allowed to watch that channel, but I guess one of the orderlies changed it when everybody was in bed." Aaron stared off into space. "It was the strangest coincidence…"

Lila said, "I don't believe in coincidence. These days I believe in miracles."

He smiled at her. "Maybe. Because the girl who was singing…she's not famous… I mean, you wouldn't know her, but I did. And I know people feel this way about certain songs, but I swear she was singing right to me."

Suddenly from behind them came a loud crash.

Lila, Aaron, and several of the patrons turned to see Christian standing in front of the double doors to the kitchen. His jaw was slack, his hands open, and a catastrophe—the results of a dropped bussing tray—lay sprawled at his feet: broken plates, spotted red napkins, a generous scattering of basmati rice.

He stared at Aaron. Was it possible? Did he dare believe it?

Lila seized the moment. "This is my young friend…"

"We've met," said Christian.

"Honestly," said Lila. "I don't know why I bother to introduce you to anyone."

Aaron slid off his barstool. "I went by your place."

"I couldn't stay there," said Christian. His eyes filled with tears. "I thought you were dead."

Aaron opened his arms.

Christian staggered through the mess on the floor.

Lila looked from one man to the other. Their faces glowed with love and tears. "Is this? Wait a minute, this isn't…"

Aaron fell into Christian's arms. They embraced tightly for a moment, then gently, tenderly pressed their lips together.

"Oh, my," murmured Lila as their kiss become more passionate. "I see." She discreetly glided toward the kitchen. When she passed a booth where some older men raised their eyebrows at the sudden loss of decorum, she casually leaned over to whisper to the most shocked of them: "He's a great tipper."

"Ooh…" the man said, nodding. Of course: Everything made perfect sense.